Jamie's Got A Wand

Southern Fried Sass
Book #4

by
Julia Mills

Welcome to Hairy Wart, Luuueeesiana.
The tofu is southern fried, and the Soul
Food is vegetarian ~
'Cause it's just not right to eat your
friends.

JOIN THE CLAN!

Wanna keep up with all my crazy? Have fun? Win some cool prizes? Get exclusive excerpts of upcoming books? Sign up for my newsletter at JuliaMillsAuthor.com. Be the FIRST to see new covers, sneak peeks, and, best of all, ADVANCED COPIES OF ALL MY BOOKS and REVIEW COPIES OF ALL MY AUDIOBOOKS!!! Join the group! Julia's Mills' Fan Club on Facebook! I absolutely LOVE stalkers! Follow me everywhere!

Website
Facebook
Instagram
TikTok
Pinterest
BookBub
Goodreads

ACKNOWLEDGMENTS

Edited by Em's Editing
Proofread by Book Nook Nuts
Beta Read by Linda Levy

To Tammy Payne, you are truly a sister of my heart. You are a blessing that I thank God for every day. Love you to the stars and beyond.

JAMIE'S GOT A WAND

Bubble, bubble, who the hell asked for a bubble?
We're off to the Swamp, a nasty hex to tromp.

Wanda the wand is rarin' to scoot, and the crazy Wolf is a root-a-toot-toot. (Sorry, rhyming's not my thing. Talk to Daisy. She's the danged poet.)

Grab your boots, your magic, and a big can of bug spray, I'mma need all the help I can get to keep this evil at bay.

The Dragonettes are out like a light with no little Prince Charmings in sight.
Yes, there'll be Gators, but no worries, they've all been fed.
Even that nasty little redhead,
Nannette and her crazy brother, Ted.

P.S. If you see Dash, tell him to get his Slothy butt to the Swamp!

PROLOGUE

"Now, *that* was one helluva opening night!" Tossing the terry rag I'd used to clean the bar top into the hamper like I was an All-Star NBA forward at the buzzer of game seven of the finals, I cheered, "Hell yeah!" Then, just because I'm me, did a little boot-scoot to the music blaring from the jukebox.

"Guess Hairy Wart was *seriously* ready for the Hairy Hangout to reopen?" Thibaut (Pronounced *T-boe* for y'all who aren't from around here, like me.) snickered with a grin, letting me know how very pleased with himself he was.

To be honest, I'd had a crush as big as Cupid himself on that sexy Wolf from the moment he rode into town. (Dude, has a custom Harley that is one fine piece of machinery.) So smitten, I even convinced my sisters to help him fix up the burnt-out shell of a bar Miss Bunny said had been an eyesore on the main strip of our little town for more than ten years.

Then, pretty much par for the course where my luck is concerned, I figured out he wasn't my True Fated Mate. But every cloud has a silver lining. We ended up best buddies instead of lovers. (Just so's ya' know, I did *finally* find out who my Mate is. To date, he's slinked off to parts unknown after the shit hit the fan a few months ago. As far as I'm concerned, he can damn well stay in whatever tree he's hanging from. Dumb, lunk-headed, buttface.)

Giving Thibaut a nod, I teased, "Yeah, I guess we did alright. Lord knows we were busier than a cat coverin' crap on a marble floor."

And I had the aches to prove it. The bottom of my feet were on fire from runnin' around like a chicken with my head cut off when my arms decided to join the 'Kick Jamie's Ass' party. Hurtin' like a nasty son of a bitch, they felt like overcooked, dried out, then heated up again, cheap, bagged noodles.

I'd been mixin' drinks and pullin' the handle on eight kegs all damned day and most of the night. Hairy Wartians, as I called them, damn sure liked to drink. Yep, I was almost too tired to think, but I still had to give Thibaut as big ole rasher of Witchy shit.

"Maybe there'll be a *real* crowd tomorrow night," I teased with a straight face and made-up snotty attitude. Watching the shock wash over his face, I added, "Unless you scared everybody off, ya' grumpy old asshole."

Getting my joke and snickering out loud as he threw a dirty bar towel at my head that I caught in midair, he ended up laughing out loud when I added, "Missed my face by a mile. Ya' know ya' gotta do better than that in ya' get one over on the Jamie Mac, Wolfboy."

"That's Wolf*man* to you," he teased, picking up a chair and turning it over onto the nearest table. "You're a serious pain-in-my-ass, but I don't know *how* I'm ever gonna thank you and your sisters for helpin' get this place up and runnin' in record time. Havin' to pay cash upfront to old man Mooney damned near took every last penny I had saved."

"Well, you already let Rosie and Benny use your daddy's cabin in the woods and sent Kerrirose and Freddie to some cosplay thingamajigger they were dying to attend."

"Yep!" He grinned. "And Daisy and Mal are all tucked up in the mountains and I got the wood to make the cradle for Faith and Beau's baby."

"Dude, you are on. the. ball."

Making a show out of shining his nails then blowing on 'em, he snickered, "And... I have something *fun* planned for you, my friend."

"Oh no, Mr. Howl-At-The-Moon," I scoffed almost without giggling while continuing to wipe the shiny wooden bar. "You're kinda 'fun' scares the bejeezus outta me." Unable to hold back, I laughed out loud which had him barking right along.

Catching my breath, I added, "In all seriousness, you've done more than enough. It's me who should be thankin' you for givin' me a job. Never thought about bartendin' but I love it." Letting out a tired breath, I went on, "And, well, I've been thinkin'..."

"That's new for you, innit?"

"Shut up, T." I flipped a coaster like it was a frisbee in his general direction. "As I was sayin', this whole detective thing just isn't for me." Spinning a napkin embossed with the logo of my favorite beer in circles by the corner, I sighed, "I mean, havin' a family is better than sliced bread and homemade raspberry jam and walking right into a family business is crazy awesome. It was always just me and mom. Every single one of my crazy-ass sisters are the best. I love 'em a little more every day."

Shifting from one foot to another, I bit my bottom lip

before going on. "I mean, I know Faith really wants us all working at Southern Fried Sass, but I'm not the paperwork-filling, listen-to-old-ladies-talk-about-their missin'-cats, findin'-kids-who-are-sneakin'around-drinkin'-beer-and-smokin'-cigarettes-while-hiding-from-their-helicopter parents-kinda girl. And, good Goddess, do *not* get me started on Portia."

"I hear ya' there, Girl." Thibaut stopped what he was doing and looked over his shoulder with a that-girl-is-crazy-as-a-bed-bug look. "I finally had to pretend like I liked fellas to get that peculiar Pink Pixie to leave me alone. She's one scary little girl with the magical power to back it all up."

"Dude, who are you…"

"Jamie…"

The barely audible sound of my name coming from somewhere under the beer coolers had me stopping midsentence and blurting out, "You hear that, T?"

"Hear what?"

"Jamie! Jamie MacElfresh!"

A little louder and undoubtedly more insistent, the voice yelled again. Dropping to my knees, I hunkered down and put the side of my head right on the floor. (Oh stop! I knew it was clean. I'm the one who mopped the damned thing.) Peering under the clear glass case housing all eight, shiny-silver beer kegs, I whipped Wanda, my trusty wand and the only thing I had left from my momma, outta my back pocket, instantly pointing the tip into the darkness.

"Illuminate," I murmured, examining every nook and cranny for who or, more to the point, *what* was hollering at me. (And before you give me a whole bushel full of shit, *we* were using 'illuminate' long before that Harry wizard kid was a gleam in his daddy's eye. Also, I know he uses that other word, I'm just coverin' all my bases.)

"What the hell are you doin'?"

Bumping my head on the edge of the stainless-steel sink as Thibaut appeared on *my* side of the bar, effectively scaring the living daylights right outta me, I dropped Wanda on the floor, grabbed the back of my head, and snarled, "Gettin' a damned concussion. Ever heard of tellin' a girl before sneakin' up on 'em."

Leaning on the counter and rolling his crystal blue eyes, the Wolf scoffed, "And what good would that do? If I'm tryin' to sneak, I'm not gonna tell ya' I'm comin'. Kinda defeats the whole purpose of bein' sneaky, duddenit?" Grabbing a towel and wrapping it around a handful of ice, he added with a chuckle, "And, I wasn't sneakin' up on ya'. I was comin' to see if you'd finally lost whatever little bit of that wacky mind you had left."

"Ha-Ha-Ha." Taking the icepack, I lifted it to the quickly rising goose egg atop my head and exasperatedly explained, "I'm not playin' hide-and-sneak, someone or some*thing* was callin' my name. I swear, it came from there." Pointing at the spot where Wanda was still laying on the floor, I asked a tad more tenaciously, "You *sure* you didn't hear anything? Haven't taken up ventriloquism without tellin' me? Don't fuck with me, T."

"Darlin', you're the only dummy I know." Laughing out loud at his own then jumping backward when I slapped at his shins, Thibaut put out his hands and wiggled his fingers. "Come on, let me help you up. Then I'll see if I can find your ghost."

Getting back on my feet, I freely admit to taking a step backward. I mean, I stayed close, but I *was* freaked out, and my head hurt something fierce. Don't get me wrong, I wanted to be right there when old Wolfie found out I wasn't losing my marbles. I'm all about telling his cocky ass, 'I told you so.' I just wanted to be out of the line of fire, if there happened to be any.

Watching and waiting, I made it about ten whole seconds (Patience is not a virtue I have ever possessed.) before asking, "Well, do you see anything?"

"No, he doesn't, Jamie. Only you can see or hear me right this minute. Now stop messin' around and help me."

Spinning one way then the other, I yelped, "There! There it was again. Now, don't tell me you didn't hear that, Thibaut Mouton. It was as clear as a bell, and so loud the windows shook."

Standing up and handing me Wanda, the Wolf laid his hands on my shoulders and raised his eyebrows. Then, with all the audacity he could muster, (And that's a whole helluva lotta audacity, let me tell you.) he talked to me like all my ducks were walking backward in a crooked row with their wings covering their eyes after swimming in a barrel of whiskey. "Maybe you oughta just go home, Darlin'. I think you might've had just a little too much excitement for one day." Giving a nod towards my thumping noggin, he added, "And that bump on your head can't be helpin' matters."

Shaking my shoulders to dislodge his hands, I stepped right up to that arrogant so-and-so, and while poking him in the chest to emphasize every damn word, ground out through gritted teeth, "You. Are. An. Asshole."

"Yes, yes, he is."

Whipping his head to the side and looking down at the exact spot we'd both just checked out, Thibaut's eyes, wider than saucers and bluer than a summer sky, shot right back to mine. Brows furrowed and lips turned downward, he growled, "What the hell was that?"

Swatting his arm, I threw my hands in the air and

declared, "See? See there? I'm not ready for the looney bin. You just can't hear for shit."

The sound of tiny nails scratching the terracotta tile had us both spinning like tops then staring at the big-eared, gray-furred, long-tailed Greater Bilby known better in his human form as Billy Crankshaw. Dropping to my knees, I slapped my palm on the floor right next to the Australian mouse's head and seethed, "Were you trying to send me over the edge? Or just fuckin' with my mind? Slow night in Ratsville?"

"No and no and shut the hell up," came his snarky and straightforward reply.

"Then change back into your beanpole self so I can kick your ass all the way back to the Swamp...*in New Zealand.*"

Standing up on his hind legs and looking as irritated as I've ever seen a marsupial resembling a gray mouse with big pointed ears and a long, skinny tail look, (This was the first time, but ya' never know when it'll happen again. This *is* Hairy Wart, after all.) Billy boy snapped, "I can't."

"You *can't*?" Thibaut exclaimed. "What's wrong with ya'? It's not like you can *forget* somethin' like that."

Shaking his little head as he rolled his beady black eyes with such gusto I wondered if they'd get stuck facing the wrong way, Billy groaned, "I didn't forget, you stupid dog. I've been hexed. I *can't* change back."

"I'mma put the pointy toe of my boot right up your little rat's ass," Thibaut snarled, trying to move me out of the way to get to Billy.

Holding back one *very* pissed off Werewolf, I couldn't help but ask Billy, "You've what? How in the hell did something like that happen? I would've felt the magic, the disturbance...the somethin'." (FYI-Hairy Wart is a super-duper mystical, enchanted, supernaturally charged place. I'm not sure if it sits atop a vortex or what, but this place is kicked-up to the max. Which means, as a Witch, or anything else of the Paranormal Persuasion, if anybody so much as thinks about using their powers – the airwaves wobble and we know.)

Looking at me as if I was the one wearing fur and hangin' out under a beer cooler, Billy's whiskers twitched so fast they were nothing but a black and white blur then without warning his high-pitched scream damned-near broke my eardrums as he scolded, "I don't know, Broom Hilda!" Scurrying forward and tapping the end of my nose with his grimy paw, he added with a hiss, "You're the freakin' Witch. Get with the nose-wigglin', Endora."

"First of all, Endora was the mom. It was Samantha who wiggled her nose to use her powers." Giving the Bilby the palm of my hand as he opened his mouth to say something else stupid, I didn't miss a beat. "Secondly, run your BS past me one more time."

"Seriously? You're correcting my knowledge of pop culture at a time like this?" Billy groaned, slapping his paw to his head. "Just my luck, a hundred of y'all Sister Witches runnin' around the damned countryside and I gotta get the dim-witted dipshit."

Gripping Wanda so tightly she zapped the palm of my hand to make me loosen my hold, I snarled, "You know what, Ratface? You can take your furry ass and your gnarly little teeth right back out to that Swamp and may the fleas bite 'cha where the sun don't shine." Still contemplating turning him into something slimy that crawled on his belly, I added, "I hear Gators like fresh rodent with extra spice."

"I. Am. Not. A. Rodent." He snapped right back, waving his tiny balled-up fist at me. "And Gators are bottom-fee..."

"You better rethink whatever's 'bout to come out your

mouth," the slow drawl of none other than Hairy Wart's Sherriff and my Gator-in-law, Beauregard St. Croix advised. "My kin don't take too kindly to species-motivated slurs." Appearing through the big, swinging silver doors leading from the kitchen, he added, "Come to think of it, I don't much like 'em either."

Holding up his paws and waving 'em like he was air traffic control at DFW the week before Christmas in a freak snowstorm, the Greater Bilby stammered and stuttered then starting talking so fast every damned word ran together. "Nonononoooo,Sherriff.I'dneversaynothin'badabouty-ourkinnoryou.NeverneverneverNEVER.Iswearonmylife.-Pleasebelieve…"

Knocking back the brim of his Stetson with the knuckle of his index finger, Beau chuckled, "Calm down there, Billy boy. Don't have heart failure or choke on ya' own tongue. 'Cause ain't nobody here givin' ya' mouth-to-mouth."

Still shaking and shuddering and spluttering a whole barrel full of garbledy-gook that sounded like something out of one of the late-night horror movies my sister, Kerrirose, is always watching, Billy flopped back onto the bar and wheezed his little heart out. Seriously, I almost felt sorry for the little pain-in-the-ass…just *almost*. 'Cause in my humble opinion, Billy Crankshaw deserved to have a knot jerked in his tail and then some – every day and twice on Sunday.

Turning towards Beau as he was talking to Thibaut, I overheard, "Yeah, I was headed to Miss Bunny's for some dill pickle potato chips, thick-sliced spicy pepperoni, and mint chocolate chip ice cream."

"Faith having cravings already?" (I butted in. It's just another part of my charm.) Unable to keep from laughing out loud when Beau slapped his hand over his heart, and his eyes got big and round as he solemnly nodded, I added, "Have you decided if she's having twins or triplets or maybe more yet?"

"The hell you say!" He spat, his face turning so red so quickly I wondered if he'd forgotten how to breathe. "There better only be one little guy in there." Holding up his hands and putting his palms less than two inches apart, he added, "Like little-little-teeny-tiny-tiny. I'm already terrified, and we've got at least seven months to go."

Just to catch you up...Beau is the Leader of the St. Croix Gator Family and my sister, Faith, his Mate, is, as you might've guessed – a Witch. About now, you're scratching your head and asking, "Jamie, exactly how does that work? Are they having baby Gators? Little Witches? Gatches? Wittors?"

To that, I say, "Hush, silly humans." Then after laughing out loud at my own joke, go on to clarify - The Universe *does not* make mistakes. Without fail, She divines the perfect match for every single one of her Special, Unique, and Wonderful Creations. (Yep, you guessed it. That's all of us. The whole Paranormal, Supernatural, Witch, Shifter, Vampire, Fairy, Pixie, etc., etc., etc. Fam-Damily.)

That includes making it possible for Gators and Witches to 'procreate' (I had come up with the most technical term I knew because just thinking about any of my sisters having 'sexy time' with their Mates (Stop singing bow-chicha-wow-wow. It's beneath you.) gives me the willies. Even as I'm saying this, the hairs on my arms are standing on end, and a shiver just whipped down my spine.) and have perfectly 'normal' children. (Yes, I added the finger-quotes because normal is a so very relative term. If you don't believe that, then get your happy heiney to Hairy Wart. We'll make a believer outta ya'.)

And by normal, I mean, Beau and Faith's little bundle of joy will probably come out with pretty green eyes like her daddy, long dark hair like her mommy, and look just like any other newborn born to Mary Jo and Joey Jim Whoever at Fayette Memorial Hospital right here in Swamp Water Parish, Louisiana.

Then, one day, our little Superstar, cause that's what she'll be, might snap her finger and turn every kid on the playground into a slug or scratch an itch behind her knee and get scaly... or both - at precisely the same time. It's all part-and-parcel of the fun of Paranormal parenthood...or so I've heard.

Also, while I'm talking about family, I should tell you that I was raised by my momma, didn't know my dad, and wasn't aware I had sisters until just a little bit ago. You see, my mom was one of literally hundreds of very, *very* Gifted Witches who were hornswoggled by the man my sisters and I not-so-affectionately call Nate the Bastard.

Here's the Reader's Digest version of what we – the Children of NTB (My name for our elite group of siblings.)- have put together so far. Dear old dad sold his soul to the Devil long before he met any of the unsuspecting women he used as vessels (His word, not mine.). You're not gonna believe why he did it. Hang with me, I'm getting to that. The preview is, by all accounts still is, our Sperm Donor is dumber than a wet sack of dicks and greedier than an old hog. Hand to the Goddess, I speak the truth whether we like it or not. Better to deal with what we've been given and move on, ya' know what I mean?

It's not a pretty thought, but those of us known as the Southern Fried Sass Sisters (More on that in just a bit. I inherited the name when I got here. It's growin' on me.) have come to terms with the fact that Nate's funked-up DNA runs through our veins. We do thank the Goddess every single damned day that our mothers were 'somewhat' normal, very, *very* powerful with loads of white magic, and on the good side of the Goddess and the Grand Priestess. (Woohoo for dominant genes and good being stronger than evil!)

Anyhoo, our fartface father decided to have children with absolutely as many unsuspecting Witches as he could then hangout and wait until those children came into their powers. He would then substitute the kid's soul that was the nastiest, dirtiest, and foulest just like him for his with the King of Hell – yep, you guessed it - big, bad Lucifer himself.

If that wasn't enough, it's my theory that he planned to use each and every one of us who happened to be left to form his own mystical, magical army with plans of taking over the world – or at least as much of it as he could. Father of the year material, right? No way! Not even if he was up against Atilla the Hun, Baron Samedi, and well, Lucifer. Our Sperm Donor is hands down *the worst*.

Our collective gene pool is a muddy puddle of shits, giggles, sludge, and ugly old pond scum. I am in awe of the fact that Faith has decided to reproduce. I think it has something to do with her hunka-hunka-burnin'-Gator-love Mate, and that's cool. I respect their decision. To each his own.

However, I plan to practice the art of 'makin' a baby' lots and lots without the side effect of a little Jamie, little Dash, little Jamsh, or little Damie. That is, if I ever get over wanting to skin my sexy-as-homemade-sin Mate alive. And for me to put away my wand, he will need to show up from wherever he hightailed it to, on his hands and knees, groveling and begging for forgiveness.

Even then, I have promised myself that I will only give into his charms after being showered with love, affection, and a shitload of expensive presents. For now, I' mma finish this little bit of backstory with y'all and get on with the show. 'Kay?

Back to the recap...

As luck would have it, Aunt Dot, one batshit crazy Witch with a heart of gold and a hair-trigger temper, happened to be hanging out with some of her friends in one of the many backwater dive bars near Buttface or Asshat or *Whateversville*, West Virginia where another of my sisters, Harmony now lives - in the house she inherited from Auntie Dot.

Yes, it's true, Dot is now and forevermore one of the 'living impaired.' (Her definition, not mine.) She does, however, not subscribe to the old adage of resting in peace. She is the Ghostess with the mostest, still raising hell and wreaking havoc whenever and wherever she can.

Yes, I digressed again. Get used to it. My mind goes in seventy-eleven directions and my mouth follows right along.

Anyhoo, back in the day, she happened to hear Nate the Bastard telling his merry band of dipshits about his crazy plan to populate the earth with his Slimy Spawn. (Sure, the term is offensive but, (1) We all say it about ourselves. And (2) Most of our other siblings turned out to be, well ... umm...let's just say, drooling, moaning, shuffling flesh bags. Offense intended.)

After running home and telling Harmony's mom, Mary, who was pregnant with my awesome half-sister at the time, the two came up with the plan to banish dear old dad to CopacaNetherworld. (That's the deep dark hole stuck between Purgatory and the Pits of Hell where Witches and Wizards who effed up in epic and truly horrible ways while alive get to hang out for all of eternity and then some. Think 1960's Vegas, complete with the Rat Pack, scantily clad cigarette girls, and mobsters, where the same day repeats itself over and over, you can never get drunk no matter how many Gin and Tonics you toss down your gullet, and the food tastes like *actual* shit on an actual shingle. Colorful, but still Hell no matter how you slice it.)

Giving credit where credit is due, I have to say Dot and Mary had some real *chutzpah*. Nate the Bastard was strong all on his own but hopped up on Hades' Hellfire, he was tougher than a team of oxen and conjoined twin Sumo wrestlers all wrapped into one. What the ladies were able to achieve was freaking awesome. They are my heroes – right along with momma.

My girls were ready and waiting. Nate walked in the front door, Dot and Mary cut off his head, threw a major-kick-him-in-the-ass-make-him-see-stars whammy on his skanky hide and just like fresh lemonade on a sunny summer day – they were rid of the asshole. Our Sperm Donor was miraculously thrown into the biggest club in Purgatory, (Yes, they put his head back on. Too good for the likes of the Nate the Bastard, if you ask me. But they didn't, and that's cool.) making the world was safe from his lying, impregnating ass for what they presumed would be forever.

Of course, his Assholishness had taken some precautions. Unbeknownst to Dot and Mary, during the years after he'd made his pact with Hades and before he met Faith's mom, Nate the Bastard had been shoving a nasty little spell - one he'd whipped up in his spare time - into every gosh-blessed grimoire he could lay his grimy hands on. The curse, when found by Harmony, would brainwash her into repeating it and releasing him from Witchy Purgatory.

Talk about hedging your bets. I'm sure as the Goddess made little green apples that the bastard assumed he'd thought of everything. Why is it that genuinely awful people always come up with the most foolproof plans? Yeah, I have no clue either. Something to think about though, later, after you finish my story or while you're folding clothes or walking the dog.

Sorry that my abridged explanation turned into the Encyclopedia Britannica, but you're gonna need this information. Promise. Oh! And, I will get to the family tree - as we know it - in a bit.

Okay, back to the business, my people.

"You're gonna be a great dad," Thibaut reassured. "My mom always said it takes a village, and Lord knows with Faith's sisters, Miss Bunny, Henrietta, Granny, Jessica... oh hell, *everybody*, you've got all the help you're ver gonna need."

"Yeah, *that's* what scares me," Beau snickered, bumping my elbow with his as he winked. Hurrying on when I wiggled my nose and zapped him in the butt with a spark of magic just to be cheeky, the Sherriff sighed, "So, what's going on? I could hear Billy losing his mind all the way at the end of the street and figured I better check it out."

Opening my mouth, I didn't even get to take a breath before that weaselly little mouse-of-a-asshole jumped to his feet, scampered up my arm, across one shoulder then the other, and while digging his claws in to keep from falling, yelled, "We've been hexed! Cursed, I tell ya'! And instead of helping, Broom Hilda here is yuckin' up with you!"

Yep! Billy's a dick. A dick with an Aussie accent.

2

"You didn't even give me..."

Stopping midsentence when Beau raised a single eyebrow and glared in my direction, I wondered if I could get away with turning Billy into a worm and going fishing without getting into trouble. However, my sister's Mate is a no-bullshit-kinda guy with a badge and a gun who can run really fast.

I can't. Or, more to the point, *won't* run.

Plus, and the real reason I didn't act on my dark impulses (I blame Nate the Bastard for having them at all.) is that using magic *always* comes at a price. Especially when you're putting the revenge whammy on someone. (Think huge, flaming boomerang topped with a steaming pile of dog poo coming right at your face. Yep! GROSS! Now, you see why I shut that shit right down whenever possible. Karmic retribution is a bitch.)

Clenching one fist so tight that my nails bit into my palm while the other held onto Wanda for dear life, I could feel Thibaut staring at the back of my head as I glowered at my Gator-in-law and not-so-patiently listened.

My BFF was trying to tell me, without words, to chill the hell out. It wasn't working. Never did. Don't know why he wasted the energy.

"Alright," Beau sighed. "Since I'm supposed to be pickin' up pregnancy provisions…" (His use of air quotes almost made me crack a smile…*almost*.) "…for my beautiful wife, I'm gonna have to leave this up to y'all." Leveling his glare with both eyebrows firmly furrowing into what kinda-sorta looked like a well-groomed caterpillar in the middle of his forehead, his eyes bore into mine. "And, Jamie…" There was a pregnant pause meaning *listen up and listen good.* "…I'm leavin' *you* in charge."

The little Witch in the back of my mind stuck out her tongue, wiggled her booty, and sang, "Nanny nanny boo-boo." Then he added, "Since the others are out of town and there's no way in all that's holy I'm lettin' Faith get involved, this one's all you, Jay Bird."

And just like that, even though he used my favorite nickname, my little Witch went from happy to ticked-off and hissed, "Son of a bitch!" My balloons of happiness went *pftttttttt*, and adding insult to injury, the whisker-faced, dimwitted Bilby voiced his opinion.

"Oh, hell, no!" His piercing, nasally, million-decibel squeal slashed through the airwaves – and my brain - like a bloody machete. "You can*not* leave this up to Witch Hazel. It's too important. It's our freakin' lives! We'll all end up inside out with our asses where our heads should be and…"

"Yours already is," I spat. Slamming my fists onto my hips to keep from turning the little bastard into the pile of poop he was acting like. Unable to stop, I kept right on yelling, "You came to *me*, Turdface." Yanking the fleabag rodent off his perch on my shoulder by the tip of his tail and giving him a good shake, I railed on, "I damned sure didn't come looking for your down-under-kiwi-stinkin', slimy ass."

(Yeah, I know I wasn't making sense, but I was *irate*. Smoke rollin' out my ears, face red, magic poppin' and cracklin' and fillin' the whole damned bar, mad as a wet hen *pissed the hell off*. I could *not* have cared *less* if I sounded like I'd lost my ever-loving mind. Stuffing Billy with sawdust, poking him with pins, and practicing Voodoo on his Australian ass was first and foremost on my list of things to do. But I didn't. And, for that, I deserved a gold star. Didn't get one, but I deserved it.)

Smack dab in the middle of my bitching rage, a set of strong hands clamped around my upper arms completely messing up the picture of my 'Billy Voodoo doll' with pins sticking out of every orifice hovering in my evil little mind. Opening my mouth to cuss out my boneheaded BFF, I instead ended up shrieking, "What the fuuuuuuuuu..."

Having totally lost his mind, at least in my humble opinion, Thibaut lifted me completely off the floor and spun me around while Buttfaced Beau extracted a screaming Billy from my fingertips. But they weren't as smart as they thought they were...well, not quite any way.

The second my feet hit the floor, I did the world's fastest U-turn and made it exactly half-a-step before my 'wonderful' (Yeah, I meant that *just* as sarcastically as you think I did. Probably more.) Gator-in-law pointed his index finger at the tip of my nose and with an *almost* scary growl, ordered, "Stop right there, Jamie Lynn." (Can you believe he used my middle name? Not cool, I tell ya'. Just not cool!)

Before I could react, said Gator-in-law jerked Billy, who was still dangling from his tail, up even higher into the air. Jerking to a stop that much to my delight made the rat squeak, when both men – one in human form and one in

Greater Bilby form – were eye-to-eye, Beau seethed, "And as for you…" Pupils going from round to elliptical right as his voice dropped about two-and-a-half octaves, (Yep! You guessed it. His Gator was itchin' to pop out, and I was having one helluva good time imaginin' Billy becoming the big scaly guy's hors d'oeuvres. I know that makes me a bad, little Witch, but the rat had pushed me too damned far.) he rumbled, "Jamie's right. *You* came to her. Now, keep your damned mouth shut and let her do what she's good at."

Eyes flashing to mine, they narrowed just that much more as the muscle in his jaw twitched like a cat on a hot tin roof. "And you, dear little sister, keep your attitude in check and your wand holstered – unless you need her to battle the bad guys."

Waiting – utterly motionless - while the Greater Bilby threw an absolute shit fit just inches from his face, I knew Beau wanted me to nod, needed me to let him know that I understood what he was saying before he went on. I was also well aware that I should just do it and put an end to our standoff.

Come on, the little voice inside my head teased. *It's just a little nod. Confirmation that you heard him. You're not agreeing or anything You know Beau's always got your back. He's one of the good guys.*

No matter how right my little voice was, I'm one stubborn and sassy Witch who simply cannot give in without a little bit of a fight. So, you'll understand when I tell ya' that I didn't move a muscle while ever-so-slowly counting to thirteen. (No clue why I chose that number, but I did. There ya' have it. Simple as that. I do a whole lotta shit without knowing why. Another part of the Jamie charm.) Finally, and most definitely making sure my expression showed how much I despised giving in, I gave a single, sharp nod.

Forced to instantly bite my tongue when my sister's pain-in-the-tail Mate had the utter nerve to say, "And round up all the Dragonettes. Those little powerhouses, plus Thibaut and Billy, should be enough backup for whatever asshole thinks it's funny to mess with the Shifters of Hairy Wart," I sorely regretted having not made him wait longer.

Looking like a hundred-watt lightbulb had just gone off in his brain, he hardly missed a beat. Pulling his cell phone from the back pocket with his free hand while simultaneously setting a still wiggling Billy on the bar, Beau mostly mumbled to himself, but you can bet on the fact that we were all listening.

"Let me round up the…" Beeps and boops from his phone replaced words as I opened my mouth to say, *"You better not be callin' that good-for-nothin'-Sloth-Deputy of yours,"* when the front doors of the bar flew open and I didn't get to make my opinion known.

Screaming her fool head off as she burst into view with storm clouds and lightning in her wake, Danielle, my-soon-to-be-Sloth-in-law, shrieked, "Dashiell's gonna die! Deader than a doornail! He's gonna die! He's gonna die! He's gonna die! And he ain't gonna be comin' back!"

3

With her words still rebounding all over the bar, I forgot all about being pissed off at Billy, Beau, and most of all Dash, as I raced towards Dani. Meeting the Witch/Sloth hybrid (She and Dash share a daddy, not a momma. I know. I know. It seems to be a theme with us Hairy Wartians, but you gotta talk to Fate, Destiny, and the Universe. They're the ones with the sick sense of humor. It's Their world, we're just livin' in it.) dead center of the bar, I snapped my fingers, magicking up an umbrella just as the clouds overhead opened and the deluge began. (Poor thing had being a Sloth all figured out. As a Witch, she still had some work to do, but she's a keeper, for sure.)

Her cheeks were almost as wet as my shirt as she sobbed, "Oh my G-G-Goddess, Jamie! Yo-yo-you gotta help him. Ya' just *gotta* help our Dashshshshshshssh."

With her words ending in a hiccupping wail, I reached for her hand while saying whatever words of comfort flew into my brain. Unfortunately, my own voice started to crack as I envisioned my tall, blond-haired, blue-eyed Adonis stuck as a Sloth and gasping his last breath.

(Okay, so that was a little melodramatic, but I can be that way sometimes. And, ya' gotta remember, this whole Fated Mate, lovey-dovey crap was all brand new to me. I'm a no-nonsense, call-it-like-I-see-it-Witch. Always have been. However, since getting to Hairy Wart, becoming part of an honest-to-goodness family, and discovering my Mate, the warm and fuzzies have been coming way more often than I'm entirely comfortable with.)

"Calm down, Dani." I tried to sound like I had it all under control for her sake. "You gotta chill – at least for a minute. Right now, I can't make hide nor hair outta what's happenin'."

Suddenly sandwiched between Beau and Thibaut – who were both firing off questions like they had Tommy guns instead of lips, not to mention, Billy jumping and yapping at my feet like a miniature Chihuahua - I screamed, "SHUT THE HELL UP!"

Silence - you know the kind that's deafening and echoing and you can hear a fart ten miles away - blasted through the bar. Ignoring everything *male* in the place, I put my hands on Dani's shoulders, hunkered down from my five-foot-nine height to her five-foot-two, and looked right into her watery blue eyes. "Deep breaths," I calmly instructed. (My heart was beating a hundred miles a minute. Sweat was pouring down my back. And, my knees were knockin' together like finger-cymbals in a Mariachi band. But on the outside, I looked like I had my shit *to-gether*. That counts. Look it up.)

Rubbing up and down Dani's arms, I took breaths right along with her to the point where my head got fuzzy, my ears started to ring, and I damned near passed out. (You better not be laughin'. What the hell would it have looked like if I flopped to the floor in a big ole pile of dark-haired, dark-eyed, leather-wearing Witch right after my Gator-in-law had announced how capable I was? *Ooooooo-kay*. Y'all are right. He *actually* said I was in charge because no one else was around. Geez! Couldn't just let me have it, could ya'? Y'all are a tough crowd.)

Getting it together just about the time Dani looked like she could speak in a language other than wet and soggy sobbing, I coaxed, "Nice and slow, Sweetheart." Keeping my eyes on hers as she took a few more deep breaths then nodded that she was as good as she could be, I went on, "Tell me what happened. Slowly."

Tears came flooding right back to her eyes, but this time she kept them from falling. Still shaky but doing her best, she breathed, "D-Dash is-is... He-he's in th-the Swam-the Swamp...an-and he-he-he's st-st-st-stuck." Gasping so deeply I thought she just might inhale my favorite necklace, Dani was working hard to keep it together while I was about to scream, *Hurry up! This is my man you're talkin' about!*

Millions of questions raced through my brain. What if Dash stayed a Sloth forever and always? What if he died in his furry form? Could he die? I thought Shifters were almost indestructible. Wasn't he meant to be a Sloth? At least part of the time? Was there a time limit? An expiration date? Only so many hours as an arboreal mammal? The other as a sexy man? Was he still my Mate? Of course, he was still my Mate! Was I losing my mind? Absolutely! No damned doubt about it!

Shoving everything but Dani and what she had to say out of my mind, I cajoled, "He's in the Swamp? Is that right?"

Frantically nodding, she hiccupped, "Y-Yes. In

the...*gasp*...in the...*gasp*... Swamp." Sniffling and gulping air, she went on, "He-he's in a tr-tr-tree. He 's-he's tryin' to-to hi-hide. But she's gonna get himmmmmmmmmm..."

Ending in a wail that led right back to a whole lotta sobbing, I handed my soon-to-be-Sloth-in-law off to Thibaut, punted a shrieking Billy out of the way with the tip of my boot, and fired off a round of questions at Beau. "Who is *she*? Where in the whole Goddess-damned Swamp could Dash be? You're a Shifter, can't you tell me what the fuck's goin' on? Don't y'all have that mind-meldy-always-know-what's-happenin'-to-one-another thing? Why Dash? Why Billy? Why not you? Why not Thibaut? Why not..."

Whap! Bam! Stomp! Stomp! Stomp! Was the only warning any of us got before the front of the Hairy Hangout was torn to smithereens by a roaring, clucking, hopping, baying, thumping throng of Shifters led by one absolutely *massive*, tusk-wearing, hair-hanging-almost-to-the-floor, rough-tough-gray-skinned prehistoric Mastodon by the name of Granny Cleo.

Coming to a complete stop with the really, *really* sharp and pointy ends of her horns (*Never* tell her I called them that. She gets seriously pissed. And even in human form at four-foot-eleven and ninety-four pounds drippin' wet, she's one of the scariest anybodys I've ever met. And, she's the Matriarch of Hairy Wart, Swamp Water Parish, and the Goddess only knows what else.) less than an inch from my face, her big black eyes rolled down towards mine with immense purpose.

Anger...no, not anger - *RAGE* - with a capital R-A-G-E burnt deep in their soulful depths, pulled me in, and made it impossible for me to look away. Magic - old, ancient, and *so* powerful the hair on the back of my neck stood on end - filled the room a split-second before Granny's snarling growl cut through my brain. *"We're all stuck! Forced to Shift! Can't go back! Fix this shit right now, Jamie Lynn! It's got to be you!"* (Again with the middle name?)

"But...Wait! But...Who? What? You mean... Where? I mean... Who? Why me?"

Hopping to the front, *literally,* because she was in her seven-foot pink Rabbit form, Miss Bunny swatted me across the face with her huge fuchsia paw. "Snap out of it!" She roared. "You're all we've got! Get it..."

"Together!" Jumped in her partner in life, Hairy Wart's very own six-and-a-half-foot Chicken, Henrietta. Head pecking, her bright red-orange feet clawing the ground, with her wings flapping so furiously feathers were flying through the air, she squawked, "We're gonna die! We're gonna die! We're gonna..."

"DIE!" That last word was bellowed in a chorus of bizarre Shifter (Animal) voices – both out loud and in my brain. Opening and closing my mouth like a fish out of water, it took a good three or four seconds for me to find about six words I could string intelligently together. Just about to spit them out, Beau and Thibaut were magically forced into what looked like a very, *very* painful Shift right before my very eyes.

Bones cracking. Tendons snapping. (It sounded like the world's largest rubber bands were being stretched till they popped in quick succession then flying to bits. The words *eww* and *gross* quickly came to mind.) As if that wasn't horror-film enough, skin and viscera, blood and gore, flew in every direction.

Pop! Boom! In an eye-popping flash of light and an ear-splitting boom every little bit of both men snapped back together... in an all new order. Thibaut was on four legs and wearing fur. Beau was really close to the ground with one helluva humongous tail and a whole lotta scales. Neither was happy.

As yucky as all that was - and I assure you it was nasty, nasty, nasty – what was freaking me out the most was the eerie, creepy, revolting feel of spiders crawling over me. There was a hovering fog of shitty sorcery in the air and I didn't like it, not even one little bit.

Unfortunately, the sight of a full-sized, pissed off Gator, a snarling black and gray Timber Wolf, a punching and kicking Kangaroo, (That's Jessica. Cool chick from Australia who works at Miss Bunny's Diner. Truly frightening in upset marsupial form.) a seven-foot pink Bunny hugging a seri-ously oversized freaking-out Chicken, a howling and barking Coyote, (Meet Matt. He's another Deputy with the Hairy Wart Sherriff's office. Gorgeous dark hair and eyes and the Mate of one of my sisters. I just don't know which one...*yet*.) and let us not forget Granny Cleo, the five-ton, eight-foot, raging Mastodon pushed everything else from my brain.

"What the fu..."

The words were swiped right off my tongue as a gray furry hand grabbed mine, held on tight, and spun me around so quickly I ended up flat on my ass. Snapping my eyes to whatever idiot decided to make me look sillier than I already did, I was completely and totally dumbstruck as I took in my assailant. Like breath stolen from my lungs, words failing me like they never had before, can't look away, D-U-M-B-S-T-R-U-C-K!

"Dani?" I croaked, my throat suddenly as dry as the Sahara. "Danielle? Is...Is that...ummmm... Is that you?"

4

"**Y**es," she answered, her voice kinda smoky and a whole lot lower than before. Think Kathleen Turner in her younger days.

It was freaky and mind-boggling in a *Twilight Zone* way. Not to mention, her nose and mouth were more snout-like, and her usually lightly freckled porcelain skin was covered with a thin layer of gray, white, and black fur.

Always the one in the crowd to open her mouth and insert both feet, I blurted out, "Holy crap on a corn cob! You're a freakin' Sloth."

"Duh," came back the most deadpan answer I've ever received in all my years. (No, I am most assuredly *not* telling you how many years that is. Didn't your momma tell you it was impolite to ask a lady's age? And...no cracks about my relationship with the word lady. I'll turn you into a Greater Bilby and feed you to one of Beau's uncles right alongside Billy.) "Did you think I was gonna look like a Swan? You do know who my brother is."

"Well, ummm, no, I guess I never thought about what

you would look like in your furry form." Pausing, I hurried to add, "I've really always thought of you as a Witch."

"Even though I suck at...ummm, at ummmm, magic and mess up all the...the...what do you call them?"

"Spells?" I answered, wondering if the wires in her brain had gotten crossed when she Shifted. Dani was *always* the brightest bulb in the pack, but at that moment she was dim to flickering. Unfortunately, I didn't get to investigate as the biggest pain-in-my-booty decided to once again make his presence known.

"Damn you, Broom Hilda! Enough is enough!" Billy squealed from his place atop Granny Cleo's foot. "We're all stuck in a Shift, and the clock is runnin' out." Scampering up the Mastodon's leg, over the top of her floppy ear, across her forehead, and down her trunk so fast he was little more than a blur, the little bastard shrieked, "Get on your broom and fix this shit!"

"Yes."

"Indeed."

"Please."

"Whatcha waitin' for?"

The Shifters in attendance piped up in quick succession, confirming that they agreed with Billy – they thought I was sleeping on the job. Getting more than a little miffed, it was then I remembered...

Spinning back towards Dani, I demanded, "Who was the *she* you were talkin' about when you came bustin' in here?"

Looking back at me like hair was sproutin' out of *my* face, and six-inch knifer nails had suddenly appeared at the ends of *my* fingers, my soon-to-be-Sloth-in-law curled her cute little black nose and shrugged, "Don't remember. You sure it was me who said somethin' about a *her*?"

"Yes!" I shouted, throwing my hands in the air and stomping my foot. "You did! You really did!"

Getting nothing more than a blank stare, I twirled the other way around and jabbed my finger up at Granny Cleo, "And you did, too. Didn't ya'?"

"*No.*" Her voice in my head adamantly boomed but with a weirdly different ring to it. Less human? More... Mastodony? (You'll have to use your imagination. That's the best description I got. It wasn't growly, just more faraway, hollow...not all there.)

It was then that another piece of the funked up puzzle my life had become slammed into place...

"Son of a bitch!" Jumping forward, I laid a hand on one of Granny's tusks while gently grabbing her trunk with the other and pulling her enormous head as close to mine as I could. Looking deep into her eyes, it was just as I suspected. Dammit, I truly hated being right on this one.

"It's not *you...*" Letting go of her trunk, I gently patted the leathery skin. "...that's gonna die. I mean, the Mastodon part of you is gonna be just fine. It's the Granny part that's gonna go poof, isn't it?"

Not waiting for an answer, I opened up the part of my brain that linked with Eppie, my beautiful, iridescent white Dragonette, and mentally screamed, *"Meet me at the truck and bring your sisters. There's a shit storm brewin' in the Swamp, and we need to shut that mutha down."*

I should've mentioned earlier, but as you can see, things got away from me. Sorry. I'll try to do better. What I was driving at is, Dragonettes, not their real Goddess-given name but the one we call them 'cause we can't pronounce the correct one, are six-inch wonderfully, magnificent, Southern-Fried-Sass-ass-savin' Dragons.

Yes, you read that right. Six inches, half a foot, one-sixth of a yard – little in stature, but in *absolutely no way* small in any other fashion.

These incredible, scaled Beauties possess more power in their teeny little paws – probably just one tiny talon - than a hundred Witch Covens all mushed together and powered up for one hell of a naked night of dancing under the full moon with a few full-sized Dragons thrown in for good measure.

Y'all need to know, these little Splendors have been alive a couple thousand years or so (Remember, we do not ask a lady's age.) and were made by the Goddess Druantia with the blessing of the Universe to be the Familiars for none other than...drumroll please...US – the Children of NTB! (The sane ones, at least.) They are the perfect combination of the best parts of the magical essence of Dragons, Pixies, Fairies, and Sprites.

They assist only the *most* deserving Earthen Witches (That's my sisters and me for the time being.) because we protect all manner of creatures, both great and small. Apparently, there are lots of Dragonettes, but to date, only six have made it to Hairy Wart. Dru, the eldest and Faith's Familiar, assures us that more of her sisters will arrive when they're needed. I take that to mean when more Southern Fried Sass Witches show up.

Can you believe it? There's more us, the sane – not drooling, moaning, shuffling, brain-eating – Children of Nate the Bastard out there. Hope they like crazy, 'cause we got that in spades.

Now, as I was saying, I hollered out for Eppie before telling everybody else the plan I just happened to be making up as I went. (Okay, so I had no clue what I was doing and had sworn to my Gator-in-law not to involve Faith. I admit to wondering if my promise still counted now that Beau was scaly. My conscience said it did, dammit anyway.)

Seeing less and less humanity in the eyes of my friends and family with each ticking second, my freak-out-meter was about to blow. "Okay, Jamie Lynn, time to get your shit together." Slapping my hand to my thigh, I hissed, "Son of a bitch! Now I'm using my blasted middle name."

Spinning towards the back of the bar, I screamed out loud while doing the same in my mind, "Eppie! Where the hell are you? Break's over. We gots some asses to save."

Still no answer and my brain coming up with all sorts of things that made me sick to my stomach about why she wasn't answering, I made a beeline for the kitchen. Pushing through the double doors, I snatched my keys off the hook and reached for the knob on the backdoor. Throwing it open, I screamed out loud as I almost ran right into six-foot-six of handsomely muscled, albeit gray-fur-covered, Dashiell Broussard.

"Thank the Goddess! You're al..." And that's as far as I got before my gorgeous-even-covered-in-fur-Mate collapsed at my feet.

5

Yes. I wanted him back. Yes. I wanted him groveling on his hands and knees and begging me for forgiveness while professing his undying love. No. I most assuredly did not want him unconscious and barely breathing. But that was how I got him, and as I kept being reminded, time was running out.

Using the magic the good Goddess, my momma, and all the other MacElfresh Witches gave me, I lifted Dash off the cold, hard ground and whisked him to the couch in Thibaut's office. Making sure he was comfortable and still breathing, I gave in, grabbed my cell phone out of my pocket, and scrolled until I found Faith's number.

Praying that Beau wouldn't kick my ass, or worse yet, eat me as a late-night snack, my thumb hovered over the send button. Taking a deep breath, second-guessing myself up one side and down the other, I never got a chance to press the button as big, strong, furry arms wrapped around me from behind.

Shocked silent, something I can assure you rarely – if ever – happens, I spun in those very same arms until I was looking into the gorgeous blue eyes of my Mate. "But how? You were just... Oh, screw this shit."

Slamming my lips to his, not giving a crap that he was Slothy, I kissed my man with everything I had in me and then some. It was a total mind-blowing explosion of all the feel-goods. Heat, passion, love, (So? It's true and poopin' my drawers scary as all Hell. I love the man.) and a need to be one with the person I knew deep down in my heart of hearts was the one for me.

Images, slow and flickering at first, speeding up little-by-little until they became a movie of my memories with Dash wound through my consciousness. As brief as they were, those recollections were seriously powerful. This may have been our first real-in-the-flesh-not-just-a-peck kiss but being the Mate of a Shifter had one *ah-mazing* benefit – *dream sharing.*

The first time it happened, I freaked out. Thought Freddie from *Nightmare on Elm Street* had come to carry my happy ass to the other side.

Feeling someone in your mind, in your dreams, is fucking unnerving when you know it's coming. So, just imagine being all snuggled up in bed, snoozing like a little baby 'cause the Sandwoman had just come and tucked you in and get a shock like that.

OH! CRAP! Here's a real quick look at a branch of my family tree. Daisy, my gorgeous red-headed-mated-to-a-Bear-named-Benny-whose-also-the-best-damned-baker-in-the-whole-world, is the daughter of none other than the Goddess Cassandra, the Deity humans call the Sandman. (I know. I was open-mouthed-gawkin' shocked, too.)

But, everything kinda made sense. Although I got here at the tail-end of things, I admit to wondering why Daisy was always sleep-walking through the day, then wide-eyed and bushy-tailed the second the sun dipped under the horizon. It was all because her momma is literally the freakin' Goddess of Dreams with the most excellent cover story of all time. (Once she found her True Fated Mate, she was able to be up any time of the day or night, but before that my girl was a Daytime Dreamer.)

Think about it. Everybody's just as sure as they can be that the Sandman is a tiny, little, gnome-like dude in need of a nose-job, who puts people to sleep with sparkly dust and gives them sweet dreams. But in all actuality, she is a *she* and GOR-GE-OUS. Like, could be a supermodel beautiful. Not to mention, sharp as a tack – MENSA smart with the ability of Prophecy and Foresight that is wicked crazy cool.

The only fault I could find, if it's a fault at all, is that she was hornswoggled by Nate, just like my mom and all the others. Then again, that Bastard is a silver-tongued demon – *literally and in every way possible.*

Soooooo, back to my story. I was fast asleep, not really dreaming, just falling deeper and deeper into some seriously stupendous zzzzz's when something flashed just outside my peripheral vision. Shit like that freaks a person out when you're awake and in the real world, in your mind, when you think you're asleep – it's *cuckoo-banana-pants-insane.*

Charging towards the invader without a single thought of who it might be or what it could do to me, I railed, "You better give your heart to Jesus, 'cause your ass is mine, Motherhumper."

The closer I got, the clearer the blurry, wiggly-wobbly image became -tall and broad with really defined muscles. The little Witch in my brain screamed, "Stop! Halt! Put a fuckin' pin in it. You're gonna get us killed!"

"Shut up!" I yelled back. (I know you think it proves that I have not one iota of the sense the good Goddess gave a

goose because I was not only talkin' to a voice in my head that was essentially me, I was also answerin'. However - and this is very important - Granny Cleo says it's okay to talk to yourself. You can even answer. But - and this is one helluva 'but' - if you say, 'huh? Or 'pardon me?' It's time to call the people with straight jackets. You need an extended stay in a padded room. So there!) *"I' mma kick this son of a bitch outta my head and all the way into next week."*

From one raging, running footstep to the next, the entire scene changed. Instead of running through a sparkly, fantasy land of my own making, I was jogging through Sleepy Critter Meadow (Hairy Wartians are truly imaginative when naming anything and everything.) *just this side of Gator Perch in the middle of the Swamp.*

Sun shining bright, flowers blooming, I could hear what sounded like a waterfall and knew something super freaky was at work. No waterfalls in Swamp Water Parish.

Not giving a good how-do-ya'-do and getting madder by the minute, I demanded, "Turn around, Asshole! I need to see the face of the dick I'm sending to Hell."

In the snap of a finger, the image cleared. Soft blond hair, broad shoulders that made my fingers tingle with the need to touch them, and best of all, the sexiest ass in all the South was right in front of me. So damn good it made me like watchin' him walk away almost as much as I loved gazing into his beautiful blue eyes.

Unable to stop the speeding locomotive that I'd become, I wailed, "Daaaaaaaasssssssshhhhhhh!"

Turning with a grace that completely contradicted his big, muscled body, my Mate gave me the hottest, panty-wettin' grin, opened his arms wide, and winked with a special little twinkle in his eye that sent shivers down my spine. Jumping into his embrace, my body melded to his just like those crazy authors describe in their mushy romance novels.

"Hey there, Jay Bird." Chest-to-chest, his breath on my cheek raised goosebumps all over every single one of my curves as his deep baritone rumble had my nipples standing at attention and pushing against his pecs creating friction that set my body on fire.

"Hey yourself," I breathed, so wholly turned on that all I could think about was getting Dash naked and having my wicked Witchy way with him.

Grinning like a man who knew what he wanted; my Sloth didn't waste a minute. Lips on mine, fingers massaging my ample behind, that man knew what he was doing in all the right ways. Legs wrapping around his waist, just like they knew what to do, I opened completely, trusting my man to take the wheel and get us where we wanted to go.

Needing to look in his eyes, to make sure I hadn't lost my mind, I pulled my fingers out of his silken hair, grabbed his shoulders, and very, very reluctantly broke away from our kiss. Holding tight, Dash groaned, "Oh, hell no, you're not gettin' away from me now."

"I just have to know this is real."

Pulling my body so close to his that I truly believed we were one, my Sloth growled – a low-in-his-throat-do-not-screw-with-me growl. Pupils dilated. Nostrils flared. And still, he held me closer. So much so that I was sure we'd be fused together. (And no-way no-how did I care. Stuck to my man is where I wanted to be.)

Then all motion stopped. Dash stood utterly still, looking so deeply into my eyes that the part of my soul I hadn't known was missing until I met him slid into place.

Hearts beating as one, time seemed to stand still. We were in a world of our own making, and everything was perfect.

"I love you, Jamie MacElfresh. I mean love you all the way

through, inside and out, no exceptions, no exclusions, just love you so bad it hurts. I've loved you from the first time I saw you and will love you forever and ever amen. We're gonna be together in every way possible, but right now, in this place, I'm gonna love you like tomorrow might never come." And with that, he slammed his mouth to mine.

Walking us backward, deepening our kiss, Dash's magic strengthened, filling the air around us a sure sign everything around us was changing. Sliding down his body when he loosened his grip on my behind, I knew I was right as the mattress touched the back of my knees.

Sliding his hands under the soft, worn cotton under my favorite Iron Maiden T-shirt, the feel of his skin against mine sent currents of pure sexual electricity careening through my body. Then his hand closed over my hardened nipple, and he gently massaged my more than ample breast, and every single thought flew right outta my mind.

Pulling the soft cotton over my head without letting go, my Mate looked down at my almost-naked body with a gaze of pure love and a whole lotta good old-fashioned lust. Empowering. Strong. Sensual. Sexy as all get out. I felt it all, and it was all because of my Sloth.

To know the man I loved (Yeah, it was time to get over it and admit that I loved him. Even a sassy, southern Witch like me has to give in when the time is absolutely perfect.) *like something out of a fairy tale felt the same damn way for me, just filled my little partly gray soul with a whole bushel load of peace and happiness.*

For the first time since my momma went to the Big Coven in the Sky, I knew my place in the Universe- right beside the sexiest Sloth the Goddess ever had the good graces to divine. There was not even a single doubt in mind that anything or anyone would ever come between us. Our Mating was Fate, Destiny, kismet, alignment in the stars, and the Universe's design, and the Goddess' will, all rolled into one.

Sharing the same single thought, our lips once again met. This time there was absolutely no slow burn. We exploded, imploded, caught a spark and went up in huge, glowing, crackling flames.

Love, passion, desire, need, and a hot lust filled us both. The fabric at my waist pulled tight right before Dash ripped the panties from my body and tossed them to the side. Hands right back on the globes of my ass, he lifted me off the ground and pulled me tight to his body, forcing me to wrap my legs around his waist.

Spinning us around, he took three giant strides before my back touched the cool, flat surface of a wall I hadn't known was there and couldn't care one way or the other. Lips and body leaving mine for less than a second, the sound of tearing fabric made me smile, and when he returned to me, the feel of his hard, muscled skin against mine made it hard for me to catch my breath.

His calloused hands seemed to touch not only my body but my soul. His hips pushing against mine held me in place, forcing his erection between the wet, swollen lips of my pussy.

Rolling his hips, the head of his cock teased the tip of my engorged clit with every move, making me shake and shiver in his arms. The longer our erotic dance continued, the higher my excitement grew. Proof of how much I wanted Dash wetting the inside of my thighs and the front of his.

Kissing my jaw, down my neck, and across my chest, Dash's fingers gently dug into my hips, lifting me higher up his body. Moaning at the loss of contact between my legs, my Sloth wasted no time latching onto my extended nipple and lightly biting down.

Shivering in unison, the sensations of every erotic motion was *overwhelming and wonderfully mind-blowing. Sliding his right arm around my waist, while his left hand made its way south, he simultaneously took as much of my breast into his mouth as he could.*

My thoughts, his thoughts, our thoughts flowing through the magical bond only Mates could share solidified our unbreakable union. The tips of the fangs of his Sloth rested lightly against my sensitive skin, teasing me with what was to come while he slid first one, and then almost immediately, two fingers deep inside me. Thank the Goddess for the strength of a Shifter, because no other man could've held me against the wall with just one arm while finger fucking me with the other.

Working their way in and out, increasing their speed on every pass, his nimbler digits bumped my excited clit, rubbing that special bundle of nerves deep inside my core that made my eyes cross and body crave what only he could give me.

Soon, two fingers became three. Riding his hand like a cowgirl at the rodeo, my body – heart and soul - searched for the orgasm barreling down upon me. Rubbing circles over my clit with the thick pad of his thumb, Dash pressed harder at every turn.

"Look at me, Jay Bird. I need to see the pretty eyes of the woman I love."

Eyes snapping to his, the world stopped on its axis as the true depth of his all-encompassing love shone directly into my soul. Pushing his fingers deep inside, he expertly teased my swollen clit with the palm of his hands as his gaze bore into the depths of my very being. At the perfect moment, when I thought I might spontaneously combust and be happier for it, Dash bent all three fingers, working the bundle of nerves at my core until I was flooded with so much pleasure, I damned near lost consciousness

Coming over me in endless waves of ecstasy, love, and an all-encompassing peace, my orgasm went on and on with my man continuing to slowly move his fingers in and out. Spent, happy, and more contented than I ever knew possible, I slid down the wall thankful that Dash's arm was wrapped tightly around my waist.,

Falling against his chest, I cuddled and kissed my amazing Mate as he took us to the bed. With his erection touching my thigh, it was as if the last twenty minutes hadn't happened. My body jumped to attention, ready to please its perfect match in every way.

With plans of my own to show my Sloth exactly how much he meant to me, I let him lay me on the bed, waiting almost patiently while he did the same. No sooner had his back touched the mattress than I pounced. Straddling his thighs, I carefully took his extremely hard cock into my hands, working one upwards towards the swollen head, while the other glided gently downward, squeezing at the base before repeating the action.

Eyes rolling back in his head, I smiled so widely my cheeks ached as Dash fought to maintain his control. Breathless, after three tries of trying to speak, he finally wheezed, "Oh my Goddess, Jay Bird. Oh my..."

Grin widening all the more, I worked his erection through my fists just a bit faster, effectively cutting off whatever else he was about to say. Sliding my butt down his legs until I was lying on my stomach, I positioned the tip against my lips, lightly breathing across the slit. Back bowing up off the bed, it was music to my ears as my Dashiell roared my name. Loving the effect I had on him, I licked him like a lollipop, savoring his uniquely warm and salty flavor as a drop of precum hit my tongue.

With my lips hovering, ready to take all of him into my mouth, the promise of untold pleasure within our grasps, I whispered my promise to him, "Love you, Dashiell Broussard. From the top of my head to the tip of my toes and everywhere in-between. You're the peas to my carrots, Baby. I never ever wanna be without you."

Reluctant to end our kiss, but knowing I had to take care of whatever or *whoever* was threatening our happy little Hairy Wart, I pulled away from Dash. Taking a deep breath as I forced my eyes open, I was ready to tell my man how overjoyed I was that he was okay when a raspy, ominous, downright creepy voice taunted, "Damn, Jamie Lynn. You sure know how to welcome a guy to town."

6

"Vincenzo Vinanucci," I hissed, wishing for some extra strength mouthwash (Laced with Draino.) and a toothbrush the size of my fist. "What the fuck are you doing here?"

Sensing the danger standing before me in black leather, slicked-back hair, and way too much cologne, Wanda whipped out of my pocket and jammed her handle into my palm. Vibrating with the need to zap the stupid son of a bastard (Not Nate. That would make me throw up on my favorite boots. Vincenzo just makes me sick to my stomach.) back to whatever rock he crawled out from under, the culmination of centuries of MacElfresh magic aimed the full strength of its power at the most twisted Warlock I'd ever had the misfortune of dating.

"I'm here, for you to apologize. Then I can take you back."

Eyes darting to Dash, who was still wheezing on the couch where I'd left him, I snapped my glare back to Vincenzo and snarled, "What have you done, Dickhead?" Throwing my arms open wide, I growled through gritted teeth, "This whole damned mess has your putrid stink all over it."

Evil grin widening but still not reaching his coal-black eyes, he took a threatening step forward and held out his hand. "Whatever do you mean, my lovely?"

Knocking his hand out of the way as I lunged forward and pushed up on my toes, I poked the asshole right in the chest. "I'm not your lovely. I'm not your anything. Now, stop this shit right now, or I'll..."

"You'll what?" He spat, the façade of anything friendly and reasonable melting away. Popping his head forward like a Cobra, he seethed, "You'll make me pay? You'll kick my ass? You'll zap me with your little wa..."

Taking over at the perfect moment, Wanda guessed what the little fucker was about to say and beat him to the bunch with a bitch-slap all her own. Throwing a steaming, sputtering ball of puce green magic packed with all the hatred she knew I felt for the piece of shit, my wand hit Vincenzo right in the chest.

Not waiting to watch where the asshole landed, I magicked Dash into the bar with the others and threw up the strongest barrier of enchantment I could whip up around the whole damned thing. Hitting the backdoor running faster than I ever thought I could, I let out a stream of curse words bad enough to make Lucifer blush when I saw the burnt-out remains of my little red pickup.

"He'll pay for killin' you, Rascal. I'll take every scratch, dent, and ash straight outta his worthless hide," I called over my shoulder. (Yes, I named my truck. Rascal is a man...the first real man I ever had in my life. I love him. And if there's a way to fix him, I'm damn sure gonna do it.)

Racing down the street, passing bunches of Hairy Wartians, also stuck in their Shifts, and each acting more 'animal' than usual, I vowed to return the entire population back to normal. Making a quick right at Miss Bunny's Diner, I slid through the gravel then zipped up the steps to the offices.

Busting through the front door of the Southern Fried Sass, I was already hollering at the top of my lungs, "Eppie! Dru! Fflur!"

Taking a breath because running is not my thing and doing it all the way down Main Street and up a million or so steps had left me wheezing like a '52 Chevy with clogged valves, (Yep! Know a thing or two 'bout cars, too. I keep tellin' y'all I'm one cool chick. Someday it'll sink in.) I went right back to screaming my fool head off. "Taffy! Laire! Rosse! Where the hell... *gasp* ...is...*gulp-gasp*...everybody?"

"Are you trying to wake the dead or just taking roll call at the top of your lungs?" Appearing out of thin air, our office assistant, Portia, the most petulant, pink-haired, Pearlescent Pixie from the Peaks of Mt. Percival, sniffed.

Having never before seen her tears in her eyes, much less showing any emotion other than sarcasm, I stopped short and blurted out, "What happened? Who died?"

"Oh, my great Goddess," she wailed, the high-pitched twitter of her voice making my ears ring. "They're not dead. Oh no, no, no, no, nooooooooooooo. They just cannot be dead. But I can't wake them up. I just can't. I can't. I've tried everything. All they do is sleep." Rushing forward, Portia grabbed my hand and squeezed so tight I heard the bones crack before hauling me across the entire length of the Southern Fried Sass office and into the vast room my sister Freddie called The Lounge. (I call it The Hideout because it's where I hide from everybody when I'm forced to be there.)

Damn near running into the back of the four-foot-four-inch Pixie, I dug my heels into the wood and snarled, "You need brake lights, Por… What in the holy hell?!"

Gaping at all six of our little scaled Beauties, sleeping soundly on every surface available in the Hideout, I sped forward. Shaking, patting, yelling, and cajoling, I did everything possible, to and including letting Wanda give each Dragonette a magical goose before spinning on my toes and asking a still crying Portia, "What happened?"

Changing from damsel in distress to nasty-ass nimrod in the blink of an eye, our very own Pink Pixie flew across the room, stopping only when the tip of her nose was firmly planted against mine. Fiery fuchsia bubbles throwing zigzags of electrical current in every direction exploded all around. Flashing fluorescent pink sparkles rained down from the ceiling, exploding on impact with my skin, stinging like an entire hill of pissed off fire ants.

"Don't you ever listen?" She shouted. "I told you what happened. I cried. I begged you for help." Jabbing her right index finger through the air, barely missing my ear but tangling her nail in my hair and continuing to pull, she went right on screaming, "Something is wrong, you stupid Ding-bat. We were talking, laughing, having a good time and wham, bam, thank you Aunt Pam, their eyes shut, they flipped onto their backs and one by one the only people I like in this whole stupid place floated to where you see them right now." Pushing her nose harder against mine, flames dancing in the depths of her deep rose-colored eyes, she spat, "What. Did. You. Do?"

Before I could answer and set the Pixie Pain-in-the-ass straight, the creepy sound of boot heels hitting the wooden stairs leading to exactly where we were standing at that precise moment cut through the plethora of pink Para-normal peevishness poking at my person. Grabbing Portia by the arm, I dragged her into the adjoining room, enclosing her big screaming mouth, along with the rest too, into a bubble of magical silence until I could lock the place down. Tossing Wanda into the air, I let my most excellent wand do her thing as I warded all the windows, reinforced all the doors, and finally, regrettably, released Portia from the mystical sphere.

Hands in the air, a spell on her lips, bolts of pissed of magic flew from every one of the million or so layers of her baby-pink tutu as she hissed, "Kill the Witch. Kill the bitch dead. Make her bleed. Cover her in red. Make her…"

Snapping my fingers, I grumbled, "Shut the fuck up and listen."

Lips mystically sealed shut, Portia mentally directed the scary fingers of her pissed-off Pixie magic to chase me around the room. Diving behind Rosie's desk (I prayed my overly forgiving half-sister wouldn't kick my ass into next year when she saw what a mess we'd made out of her office. Yes, I would try to fix it before she got home. Unfortunately, Pixie magic is damned hard to reverse.) Magicking up a huge white flag of truce, I hollered, "Cut the shit, Portia. I know who hurt the Dragonettes and it wasn't me."

Just like somebody flipped a switch, everything stopped. No more heat-seeking-kill-Jamie-magic, no more evil bubbles filled with stinky gas and stinging crystals, and best of all, no more curse…or at least, I was hoping.

Cautiously and as quickly as I could because Vincenzo's footsteps were getting louder, (Stupid SOB was making a game out of it. I knew he was. Dumbass could've magicked his ass up those stairs in half-a-second, but he wanted to fuck with me. Well, I had a few new tricks up my sleeve.) I stood up and released the hold I had on Portia's mouth.

Holding up my hand because I knew she was gonna

bitch me up one side and down the other, I put my index finger to her lips and whispered, "Protect the Dragonettes. I'll deal with the prick. You can kick my ass later."

Still glaring, but uncharacteristically doing as I asked, Pinkie (My nickname for Portia. Tell her, and we both die.) zipped into The Hideout, silently slammed the door, and with a blast of magic that singed my nose hairs, locked the room down tighter than Fort Knox.

Flinging magic left, right, and center, I went behind Wanda, making sure the Southern Fired Sass offices were as impenetrable as they could possibly be. Just as the loudest boot strike so far sounded on what I was guessing was the second step from the top, the hair on the back of my neck once again stood on end as Vincenzo yoo-hoo'd, "Jamie. Jamie Lynn Vinanucci, my sweet. Time to come out and play nice. We need to get home and start our happily ever after."

Biting down on my tongue until I tasted my own blood to keep from verbally, and most probably magically, ripping the stupid jerk on the other side of the door for daring to call me by his last name a new butthole, I let out the breath I was holding and with the sweetest tone I could muster, called back, "But I haven't had time to pack."

Yes. I was stalling. No. I didn't have a plan. All I knew for sure was that whatever was happening to Hairy Wart was Vincenzo's fault, and for that, I would gut him like a Pig and hang him from a tree for the vermin to feast upon.

Chuckling in the arrogant tone that always made my teeth hurt and still did in an even more spectacular way, the dirtbag mused, "Oh, Darling, don't worry about any of that. Nothing you have will be presentable at mummy and daddy's new estate. We'll stop in the city and buy you a whole new wardrobe. I don't want my new wifey embarrassing the family at our first ever celebration party."

Mummy and daddy? Did the biggest douche in all the world truly just call his parents mummy and daddy? I hadn't thought it was possible, but Vincenzo had gotten more conceited, more supercilious, and infinitely more stupid. And...to put a big fat pile of steaming horseshit on my already pooptastic sundae, he'd dissed my clothes. Asshole had to die.

But...could I kill Vincenzo without killing my man, my friends, and the Dragonettes?

I would swear she'd been reading my mind if I didn't know that she hated being in anyone's head when Portia appeared at my side and whispered, "I know what we can do."

"Holy balls!" I whisper-yelled. "Are you *tryin'* to kill me?"

"Nope," she deadpanned. "If I wanted you dead, you'd be dead." Pushing her perfectly round pink-framed glasses back up her pert, little nose, she twirled one of the hundreds of tiny, pink-hombre braids around her finger and lifted her chin towards the door in a quick nod completely changing the subject without missing a beat. "You better keep your bozo talkin', or he's gonna get suspicious. If he's not already figured out what you're tryin' to do."

Dammit, she was right. I truly hated that. But had to give her props for saving my bacon.

"Oh cool," I half-heartedly cheered. "Can't wait. Be right out. Just gotta shut off the computers, fix my hair and grab my purse."

"Okay, Honeybun. Don't keep me waiting long, or I'll have to come in and get you."

(Never had a purse, never want one. Witches, at least the ones at Southern Fried Sass, rarely, if ever, even turned the computer on. And, I never 'fixed' my hair. See, the idiot knows nothing about me, and that's the least of his flaws.)

Rolling her eyes, Portia groaned, "You really suck at this shit."

"Okay, enough of kicking a Witch when she's down," I huffed. "Do you have a plan or not?"

"I do," she grinned way more mischievously than I was comfortable with before adding with a giggle, "But you're not gonna like it."

7

She was right. I didn't like it. Not one little bit. But I didn't have any other ideas and time was running out.

The bond I shared with Dash, the link I'd closed off when he left me high and dry, was fading fast. And the one I had with Eppie was little more than a flicker. Time to do something... *anything*. Right that second. No! Sooner.

If *anyone* besides Portia had come up with the idea, I would've laughed and said, *What the hell? Let's do this.* Unfortunately, it was the Pink Pain-in-the-ass' plan. If we made it out alive, I'd never hear the end of it.

It's worth it. It's worth it. It's worth it. Gotta save Dash. Gotta save Eppie. Gotta save them all. It's worth it. It's worth it. It's...

With that mantra on a constant loop in my brain, I stood in silence as Portia covered the room in Pixie Dust, chanted some crazy-ass spell in a language she called Pixanesican, and did a twirl, a hop, and skip. Clapping her hands over her head as if she was doing a jumping jack with the jumping, the booming blast warped the airwaves. Half-a-second later, an exact doppelganger of me stood not ten feet away.

Exactly. All the freaking way. Right down to the glyphs and runes tattooed one every inch of my wand arm.

Totally amazed and completely freaked out, my heart skipped a beat, and the little Witch in my head screamed, *What the fuck? What have you done? One Jamie is almost too many!* (I have mentioned she's a bitch, right?)

Opening her mouth, Portia sassed, "Whatcha think, Hot Stuff? Good enough to fool your suck-faced stalker?"

Unable to speak, I could only nod. It was uncanny. The Pixie looked like me, sounded like me, and as scary as it was to believe – *acted like me.*

Cocking her hip, she slapped her hand on my waist. No wait, her waist? My waist? Okay. Hang on. It was *her* waist, right? Yes. Definitely. Her waist. I still had my waist. I checked to be sure. (Whew! Talk about confused.)

Doing a shimmy and shake, she shrugged, "Feels good to me. Let's get this show on the road. Your sense of style sucks and your hair is super boring. I mean, black and leather? Just black? No streaks, stripes, highlights, braids, nada? At the very least, add some pink to your wardrobe. Woulda little color kill ya'?"

Letting her criticism go unchecked because she was helping – for the first time since I'd met her and according to my sisters, the first time *ever* – I gave a quick nod. Clearing my throat, I finally found my voice and with as much humility as I had, (Like a metric ton.) sincerely showed my gratitude. "Thank you, Portia. I'll never be able to repay your kindness."

Again with the rolling of the eyes - only this time, I got a firsthand look at what others saw when I was bitchy, and I didn't like it at all - the Pixie made the shooing motion by flittering her fingers and sassed, "Oh hell no, Witchy Poo. No gettin' soft on me now. We ain't friends, and we ain't partners. I just wanna save my little friends. Everybody else is the icing on my strawberry sprinkle cupcakes and helping you ain't nuttin' but a thang." (Yep. Portia got gangsta every once in a while. It was hilarious, and I usually made fun of her just to watch her sparkly opalescent skin turn bright red. But, not this time. I was being really, really good. Like gold-star good...*again*.)

Eyes glassing over with unshed tears as they flashed on the door of The Hideout, she added with a hiccupped-whisper, "I'm gonna save you guys. With the Goddess as my witness, if my name's not Princess Portia Perriwinkle, you will be back up and flying real soon."

Holy guac-a-fuckin'-mole! Another bomb dropped right on my head. Pain-in-the-ass Portia was a Princess. Something I'd have to think about after I had my man, my Dragonette, and my friends back...or maybe never. (Yeah, most likely never.)

Looking right back to me, the Pixie did that snap-and-point thing, the gesture that absolutely made me see red because Vincenzo did it too, before winking, "And don't forget, you owe me all the gory details about Prince Not-So-Charming out there."

Watching Portia open the door and walk straight into Vincenzo's arms ended up being way harder than I thought it would be. I knew firsthand how nasty he could be, and never ever wanted anyone else to experience his 'ugly side'.

Taking a step forward, ready to reveal myself from behind the thick wall of magic that made it look like the office was dark and empty, Portia's voice slashed through my brain, *"Don't you freakin' dare. Get your ass out that window, into his car, and find that damned amulet. If even one scale on those precious, sweet, irreplaceable Dragonettes' are harmed, I swear, I'll spend the next hundred years looking like you, cut your hair into a mohawk, die it electric pink, and follow around every Swedish Ska band I can find."*

Knowing damn good and well she could *and would* follow through with every threat and probably more, I whipped Wanda out of my back pocket, and once again, much to my chagrin, found myself running.

Sliding to a stop in front of the farthest window at the very back corner of the office, I used the very first spell I'd ever learned and magicked open the window. Climbing out onto the flat roof, I prayed I wouldn't break my fool neck. Heights have never been my thing. Thank the Goddess travel-by-broom went out with the Salem Witch Trials.

(About now, you're asking yourself why I didn't just *poof* myself wherever I needed to go? Well, my little non-enchanted Cutey Pie, because Vincenzo would be able to sense the use of magic, he would recognize it as mine and know the chick making goo-goo eyes at him wasn't me. The ass-faced, turdball, waste-of-space would then kill a whole lotta people I loved....and Portia.)

Shimmying down the drainpipe, I refused to look down. Literally kissing the side of the building when my feet were safely on the ground, I took off like a shot.

Skin prickling like a million beady eyes were following my every move, I took a quick glance over my shoulder.

Breathing a sigh of relief that no one was there, my eyes – along with my head- whipped back to the front, and I doubled my speed. Zipping past the dumpster, I hurdled a pile of wooden pallets, zigged around seven silver gas tanks, zagged between four piles of boxes, and stopped on a dime at the sharp corner of the historic red brick building.

One quick gulp of air, feeling pretty damned confident and ready to send Vincenzo to Hell, I peeked around the corner to make sure the coast was clear. And, because my life makes as much sense as tits on a bull, it wasn't.

Dead center of the parking lot, back to her plucky, petulant, pinktastic person, hung Portia. Upside down, at least a hundred feet in the air, the Pixie was bound and gagged with black duct tape. (The one thing Pink Pixies can't break through.) Below was a massive pit of orange, oozing, Ogre snot, the only thing that can kill a Pearlescent Pink Pixie from the Peaks of Mt. Percival.

Stalking out, I stopped directly across from a smirking Vincenzo and slid my feet shoulder-width apart. Slamming my fists onto my waist, I growled, "The only way you're gettin' out alive is through my pleasantly plump ass. Bring it on, Buttface."

8

"Tsk, tsk, tsk," Vincenzo annoyingly, and way too condescendingly for my taste, shook his head. "Let's not make this harder than it has to be." Holding out his hand, motioning for me to go to him with the flipping of his fingers, the stupid Asshole had the nerve to smile as he ordered, "Stop your hysterics. Just get in the car. I'll dispose of all these hillbillies, and we can get on with our lives."

"You'll do what?!" Stepping forward and catching Wanda mid-flight before I even realized I'd moved, I shrieked, "What the fuck is wrong with you?!" Not waiting for an answer, I just kept right on going, "I mean, seriously? Were you dropped on your head as a child? Your mom never said anything about, but then again, she's crazy as a bedbug with three heads and no legs. Goddess even knows if she'd remember. Maybe batshit-crazy is hereditary. It's the freakin' 'Force' of your family. Like the Jedis. It is strong with this one, pad-a-fuckin'-wan."

"Now, that's just wrong, Jamiekins. You know Star Wars is my favorite movie franchise. It's…"

"Shut. The. Fuck. Up." Another step forward. More Pissed. Sparks flying out of Wanda. Still screaming like a loon. "I told you when I broke up with you the first, second, third, and fifteenth time – you suck. I hate you. I never wanted to see you again. You're a control freak. Worse, you're dominating and narcissistic and horrible. People, especially me, but people, in general, do not like to be tied up in magical ropes and locked in a dungeon because they refuse to wear lilac taffeta."

Off on a tangent I can only assume was caused by the piles and piles and *piles* of utter emotional bullshit the piece-of-goblin-turd put me through for more years than I cared to think about, I took yet another step forward with my mouth going a-hundred-miles-a-minute.

"I went out with you the first time on a dare. A fucking dare from a bunch of my drunk friends. It was a joke. You're a joke, *Vinnie*." At the use of the nickname I knew he hated; his left eye started to twitch.

"I made that perfectly clear, and what did you do?" Flicking Wanda, I shot a raging bolt of fire at his over-priced, too-shiny, pointy-toed, silver-buckled, warlock-lookin' stupid shoes as I snarled, "You fuckin' hexed my ass."

Taking it upon herself to fire a bolt of fiery, fizzing, fluorescent green fart-stinkin' sorcery at Vincenzo's chest, Wanda did a happy wiggle in my hand when her spell hit its target and kept right on screaming. "Whipped up one of your nasty spells and whammied me into thinkin' I was in love with you! Who does that shit? What the fuck is wrong with you?"

Any other time, I would've been laughing my fool head off at the way Vincenzo was hopping, skipping, and zigging-and-zagging to keep from getting hit by everything Wanda and I were throwing at him, but this time, all I cared about was ridding the world of Vincenzo.

"Answer me, Asshole! Answer me!" I roared, my body shaking with rage. "You chained me in a basement!" *Zap! Zing!* A festering hex exploded, pouring angry, squirming slugs all over his head.

"You tricked me!" The dickhead hit the ground as Wanda's jinx literally shot his knees – and everything down to his feet – across the parking lot.

"You treated me like a fucking dog!" *Pow! Boom! Bang!* Three curses in rapid-fire succession. One to the head. One to the gut. One to his teeny-tiny-useless junk – and the bastard was flat on his ass on the ground.

"But... he just kept getting up. Just kept smirking. Just kept..."

"He's got the Goddess-damned amulet around his neck," Portia's snarl slammed into my brain. *"How else would a second-rate-waste-of-bought-and-paid-for-magic be able to best me? I'm the powerful Princess of the Pearlescent Pixies from..."*

"...the Peaks of Mt. Percival." I said right along with her before adding, *"That would've been valuable information a shit-ton of wasted magic ago."* (I was seriously getting the hang of the whole talking in my head thing. Would've asked for another gold star if I wasn't trying to save everybody's ass, including my own.)

"Excuuuuuuuse me. In case you haven't noticed, I'm ass over teakettle over here with lady parts blowing in the wind, black duct tape eatin' away at my skin, and Ogre snot sizzling right below me. Maybe, I thought..."

Tuning the Pink Pain-in-the-ass out, thinking it was better before she busted through Vinnie's shit-magic, I snapped the fingers on my free hand and instantly had my version of x-ray vision. Sure as shit, there it was. The source of the Vinanucci magic hanging around the Fuckface's neck.

You see, the Vinanuccis were all Kattywops – Witches and Wizards without one drop of natural magic. Basically, plain old homo sapiens with the name of an old Magical Family – not a damn thing else.

Somewhere along the line, one of their ancestors messed up in one helluva big way. Like pissed off the Goddess, the Grand Priestess Calysta, Fate, Destiny, and the Universe all that same time. (Let me tell ya', that's one big screw-the-pooch-step-in-shit fuck up.)

Those who know the story aren't talkin'. And those who don't, have made up all kinds of tales. But think about it this way. Look at all the shit Nate has done, and he still has at least some of his powers. Sure, he's in the CopacaNether-world, but the Powers That Be didn't take his *zip-zow-whammy.*

Oh, and to make matters worse, anyone Mated to a Vinanucci. Meaning - went through the ceremony and was stupid enough to pledge their everlasting soul to one of the Asswipes – lost their powers too. Also, any children they had or will have will be Kattywops, and so on, and so on. That's what that Bat-dong-faced Loser wanted to do to me!

"See that, Wanda?" I muttered under my breath, knowing whatever thank-the-Goddess-holy-bejeezus was flowing through her willow wood knew every thought I had before I even thought it. "We're gonna take one good aim and..."

And, that was the precise moment that all manner of humanity faded from Vincenzo Vinanuuci. Flicked one hand and then the other, that Cross-eyed, colossal-cocksucking-Kattywop sucked serious juice from the lump of rock around his neck and sent Wanda and me flipping and twisting through the air.

Hitting the back of Handy Hardware like I was a wrecking ball, I kinda-almost remember sliding down the wall. More than that, bits and pieces of Portia screaming like a Blue Banshee from the Bumfukit Boothills of Mt. Bloomington for me to get up and fight.

What I will never be able to forget no matter how long I live (And I will still not tell you the number of years. *Geez! Get over it, will ya'?*) is the shadow Vincenzo cast over the pile of whooped Witch I was after being whopped upside the everything by his whammy.

Or...

That moment I realized I was about to take a one-way trip to Witchy Heaven without passing Go and without collecting two-hundred dollars.

Making a production out of besting me and being the real villain I always knew he was, Vincenzo couldn't just put me out of my misery quickly. Oh, hell no, the son of a Kattywop apparently thought we were at the climax of our very own superhero movie and gave a mutha-humpin' monologue.

"Oh, Jamiekins, why do you always have to fight me?" Pacing just far enough that the rising sun would momentarily blind me before he turned back, the dipshit went on, "It is inevitable that we'll be together. It's Fate. It's..."

"It's utter fucking bullshit!"

A primal roar, unlike anything I'd ever heard, cut off whatever the hell Vincenzo was about to say. Immediately followed by snarling, gnarling, and gnashing of teeth. Then screaming, wailing, and ripping of flesh. Followed by blood and guts flying through the air, and finally, a grand finale of big, strong, furry arms lifting me off the ground.

"Son of a bitch," I groaned in pain.

"Stop! Lay still." Came a gruff, almost human command. "You'll make it worse."

"Fuck that," I moaned, patting his face as the fur faded. "This time, I 'mma makin' sure."

9

___

"I'll just never forgive myself," Eppie fussed, setting the umpteenth mug of herbal tea on the coffee table. "You could've been killed. I'm meant to protect you. That's it." Her little paws flew in the air as she flitted back towards the kitchen of Dash's house, turning around and continuing her journey backward as she announced, "I'll just never let you out of my sight again."

"Wait just a..." My handsome Sloth tried to contradict before Portia chimed in, "I agree, Eppie..."

At that point, Wanda and I were about to zap her in the wazoo when the Pink Pain-in-the-bootay gave me a side-eye wink and added, "But, maybe we should let Dash take care of her for a week or two."

Stopping mid-air, my little scaled Beauty's eyes got big, and her cheeks turned the cutest shade of pink as she gasped, "Oh my...well, yes... I'm sure you're...Well, that's to say, I guess..."

Appearing all around her, the other five Dragonettes teased, an abundance of sisterly love flowing all around as

Fflur chuckled, "Trust me, you want to give the newlyweds lots of 'alone time.'"

"You know how newly Mated Witches can be," Laire snickered.

"And, I've heard Sloths can be very amorous," Dru giggled, her thick Scottish brogue getting even more of a lilt.

Not to be left out, Taffy and Rosse sang in unison, "Jamie and Dashiell sitting in a tree. K-I-S-S-I-N-G."

Slapping my hand on my forehead, I worked hard not to bust out laughing as I shooed, "Enough, you crazy band of goofballs."

Reaching for my hand, Dash's voice whispered through my mind, *"Are you sure you're okay?"*

"I'm fine," I sighed. *"Stop worrying."*

But to be honest, I loved it that he was worried. Hell, I loved him something terrible-awful, wonderful-good. He was mine, and I was holding on with both hands.

"I have to ask again…"

Everyone in the room groaned. Mostly because I kept asking the same questions over and over. In my defense, it had only been two days since I'd had my brains scrambled. What did they expect?

Ignoring the grumbles, I went right on, "How did you break Vincenzo's spell?"

"Because you were about to die," every single being in the room answered in unison, with more than a little attitude in their collective tone.

Putting both palms up to all of them, I huffed, "Fine. I'll let it go. I just…"

"No, you won't," Miss Bunny's smoky contralto sounded through the screen. Opening the door, she came right on in with Henrietta close behind. "You'll keep asking and wondering and fussing till you figure it out."

"Probably," I shrugged.

"You just gotta know that the Goddess and the Universe are never gonna let True Fated Mates get killed if there's a way to fix it."

"And there was no way, the Powers That Be were gonna let a Kattywop like Vincenzo get over on y'all," Portia added. (I admit, the Pixie was kinda growing on me. But, if you tell her I said that, I promise I'll turn you into a Greater Bilby and make you hang out with Billy.)

"Well, I'm just damned glad it did," I smiled, holding tight to Dash's hand.

"So are we," Henrietta beamed. "You are our hero, Jamie Lynn."

"Seriously?" I complained. "Again, with the middle name? What's a girl gotta do to make y'all stop usin' my middle name?"

As the room erupted in laughter, I couldn't help but look at all the smiling faces of just a few of the people I loved and thank the good Goddess for everything I'd been given. Of course, true to form, that was when the hollering voice of my oldest sister came blaring through the window, "Jamie Lynn MacElfresh, what in all that's holy did you do to the office?"

Grabbing Wanda, I yelped, "Hold on tight, Dash." One wish and a half a whammy later, my Mate and I were winging our way to Thibaut's houseboat as I called back, "Sorry, Faith. Love you. It's all Portia's fault."

EPILOGUE

"What do you mean, the hospital's on fire?"

"What part don't you get, Freddie?" I snapped. "The hospital? The fire? The two together?"

However, in my defense, I'd been at the very same hospital for damn near forty-eight hours delivering every form of squawking, screeching, hee-hawing, hopping, flopping, and flying Shifter known to Hairy Wart and then some. Last winter's cold snap had led to bunches of pregnant mommas, and the upcoming Blue Moon was bringing all those babies to Swamp Water Parish faster than any of us were ready.

"Dude, you need to get laid," my stuck-in-the sixties-hippie-half-sister-with-one-pink-ponytail-and-the-other-purple sassed.

"What the hell, Freds? Rude much?"

Shrugging, she quipped, "You've been right down rude since before we went to ComicCon. That's like our Nirvana, Kerrirose. You were uptight there, and you're uptight now." Blowing a bubble from the wad of gum she was perpetually chewing then popping it with the tip of her finger, she sucked the gunk back into her mouth and added, "Ergo, you need to get laid."

"Yeah, okay," I growled. "Sorry to bring ya' down, Sis." Grabbing my jacket and waiting until my bright pink Dragonette, Laire landed on my shoulder. "Sorry, I want to wait for my True Fated Mate instead of doing the wild thing with every hairy, scaly, and fanged Joe Bob, who looks my way."

Truth was, I'd been waiting for my Mate since the day I turned sixteen. No, I never planned to reveal that to anyone, but it was the truth, nonetheless.

Being with the one in all the world created just for me, having babies, living happily ever after – that seemed like paradise to me. After growing up in a Commune full of female Witches, then finding out my dad was Nate the Bastard, do you blame me for wanting my only little fairy tale?

Out the door, through the gate, and onto the sidewalk, I knew Freddie was right behind me, but I refused to acknowledge her. Don't get me wrong, I loved all my sisters and Winifred was no different, I was just irritated, and she was handy for me to take it out on. (Yep! I was being a Witch with a capital B.)

Seeing the pillars of smoke, I snapped my fingers, zapping Laire and myself to the farthest corner of the parking lot near the woods leading to the Swamp. Looking around, I could see where the nurses and orderlies had cordoned off different areas to match the various departments in the hospital.

Making a beeline for Maternity, I checked on Kathleen Cougar and her six new cubs, moved onto Debbie Deering and her brand new fawn triplet, and had just made it to Ophelia aka Opie Banksmere and her quadruplet Otter pups – all girls, I might add – when an overwhelming sense of déjà vu crawled up my spine. Whipping my head to the side, I saw the firemen fiercely working to put out the fire with Granny Cleo helping by shooting water out her big, ol' trunk. Snapping back the other way, Freddie almost scared the life out of me by landing not two feet from where I stood.

"Are you tryin' to kill me?" I snapped, still pissed at what she'd said before.

"Nope, just tryin' to finish our conversation, but I can see that you're still cranky. So, I'm gonna go help on the other side of the lot."

Hours passed, the fire was put out, and a makeshift hospital was set up in Father Finnegan's brand new, state-of-the-art warehouse. (No, not Father like Priest. Father like he has a gajillion, bajillion, million children, grandchildren, great-grandchildren- and the like. That's what happens when you're the oldest living Jackrabbit this side of the Mason-Dixon line.)

So tired that even my hair hurt, I filled a cup I'd borrowed from Mary Ellen Gabbard, RN (That's how she refers to herself.) with fresh coffee and flopped my well-rounded booty into the first seat I found. Letting my head fall back and my eyes slide shut, I took a long deep breath and inhaled something so smoky-sweet and absolutely succulent that my heart did a special little pitter-pat.

Scooching farther down in the chair, deciding I wasn't going anywhere as long as that tantalizing aroma was still blowing my way, I lifted to the mug to my lips.

Crash! Bam!

Flying forward, hot coffee going everywhere, but in my mouth, I screamed so loud my own ears hurt a split-second before I landed face-first in Father Finnegan's freshly tilled garden. Up on my feet, spinning like a top, I didn't even bother cleaning my face off before roaring, "Who's the fucking Bozo with a death wish?"

"That'd be me," came the sexiest voice the Goddess ever gave a man.

Slashing the dirt and mud from my eyes, I open-mouthed gaped at seven-foot nuthin' of dark-haired, green-eyed, bare-chested man. Unable to speak, barely able to breathe, I stood there like a muck-covered mute as he pulled a wadded-up T-shirt out of his back pocket, handed it to me, and profusely apologized, "Oh my Goddess, I am so very sorry, Miss...Miss..."

"Oh, that's my sister, Kerrirose," Freddie chimed in. "She's not always mute, and I'm pretty sure she's your Mate."

Kerri, Kerri, Quite Contrary
Southern Fried Sass #5
Coming 2024!

Just for You!
Later Gator, Southern Fried Sass Book 1

R*ing...ring-ring-ring...riiiinnnggg....*
"I'm coming. I'm coming. I'm com.... Son of a bitch!" I knew Miss Bunny, our landlady, the owner of the diner our office was on top of, and the leader of the HW Ladies' Prayer Circle was working up one helluva sermon just as soon as the words slipped through my lips, but in my world, hot coffee down the front of a brand new cream-colored, linen suit deserved a 'son of a bitch', a 'mother humper', and a 'shit, shit, shit', so, I figured she was lucky I stopped where I did.

Juggling the box of office supplies my half-sisters and our angsty assistant had requested, (Read that as demanded.) I bent down, grabbed my empty cup, and climbed the last three steps. Wrapping my hand around the knob, I shoved the door open and screamed, "Will someone *puhlease* get the damned phone?"

"Don't get your knickers in a twist," Portia sassed as she

sauntered into the room, plopped her butt in her chair and finally *picked* up the phone. "Bubble, bubble, are you in trouble? Not to worry, we'll be there on the double. No need to fear. No need to fret. We're Southern Fried Sass. We'll eliminate the threat. How may I help you today?"

Stopping mid-stride, left foot still in the air, I stared at the pink-haired, Pearlescent Pixie with hundreds of braids all over her head, two nose rings, and round, fuchsia-framed glasses, I mouthed, "What the hell?" To which she shrugged and giggled into the phone, "Sure Henrietta. I'll have Faith give you a call."

Rolling my eyes and groaning under my breath, I made my way into the kitchen/break room, (Another demand from the 'crew.') let the box from Oscar's Office Emporium drop onto the table and growled, "Look at this crap. Just look at it, will you?" Waving my hands up and down, making sure my half-sisters – Rosie and Daisy – got a good look at my ruined clothing, I bitched as I threw my thumb over my shoulder as if I was trying to hitch a ride on I-10 during rush hour traffic, "And who the hell told Tinkerbell she could answer the phone like that?"

"I am *not* a Tinkerbell! I am a Pearlescent Pixie from the Peaks of Mt Percival! Get it right."

Puce-colored bubbles appeared and immediately burst, fizzling like Pop Rocks thrown into a bottle of Coke. Yucky maroon smoke streamed from my fingertips, and barf-green blobs, like misshapen pieces of confetti, rained down all around the room. My boiling point was mere seconds away and all I could do was seethe through gritted teeth, "Please. Shut. Up. Portia."

"Well, I never," she huffed.

"Yeah, I'm pretty sure she has," Rosie chuckled as she kicked the door shut with the pointed, silver toe of her flaming red, four-inch heels. I have no idea how the heck she walks in those babies, but she sure does turn the male heads.

Handing her an absolutely ginormous pack of sticky notes, I grumbled, "I just don't understand why she can't answer the blasted phone. It's not rocket science." I stopped and hit the 'BREW' button on the super-dee-duper coffeemaker I'd purchased from Amazon for a small fortune before continuing. "Pick up the receiver, say hello. I mean – come on people, a monkey could do her job."

Taking a deep breath, I thought of all the things I should've or *could've* done instead of opening a Paranormal Private Detective Agency with my long-lost family. Quickly closing that door before it got completely out of hand, I added, "It's our first real day in business. Wouldn't it be nice to have a customer or two?"

"If you say so," Daisy yawned, lifting her head off the table and pushing her thick auburn curls out of her face. "I would take a day or two off just to sleep if you asked me. Maybe, we should start next week, or next month, or..." Her words faded into another yawn and her head slowly dropped back onto the stack of folders she was using for a pillow.

Thankfully, I wasn't asking her, but I wasn't getting upset with her lack of enthusiasm either. There is a reason that she is the way she is, a reason we're all the way we are. Let me explain.

You see, Rosie, Daisy, and I, along with our oldest sister, Harmony, have the extreme pleasure (Note the sarcasm.) of being the product of Nate the Bastard's sperm donations to our respective mothers.

Yes, I call my 'father', and I use the term extremely loosely, Nate the Bastard. It's the best name I could come up with. The other ladies have their own iteration of the same theme. You can only imagine the fun we have on Father's Day, but I digress...

The story we've been able to piece together since the Asshole Extraordinaire popped into Harmony's life and tried to kill her (More on that later.) is that dear old dad sold his soul to the Devil long before he met any of our moms. We don't know why he did it or what he hoped to gain, just that he was, and presumably still is, dumber than a burlap bag of dicks and greedier than an old hog – that's the truth, whether we like it or not. Better to deal with what we've been given and move on, ya' know what I mean?

It took a bit, but the four of us have come to terms with the fact that his fucked up DNA runs through our veins. We do thank the Goddess on a daily basis that our mothers were 'somewhat' normal and very, *very* powerful in the white magic, good side of the Goddess and the Grand Priestess way. (Woohoo for dominant genes and good being stronger than evil!)

Anyway, Nate the Bastard decided to have children with absolutely as many unsuspecting Witches as he could find, wait until that child had come into his or her powers, and then substitute the kid's soul for his with the King of Hell – yep, you guessed it - big, bad Lucifer himself.

Great father figure, right? Yeah, our collective gene pool is a muddy puddle of shits, giggles, sludge, and plain old pond scum. I, for one, have decided never, *ever* to reproduce. Doesn't mean I won't practice if I ever find a man that makes my wand tingle and my toes curl. But...umm, yeah...maybe we'll talk about the lack of male companionship in my life later...*much* later.

For now, let's stick to the subject at hand...

As luck would have it, Aunt Dot, Harmony's mom's sister

and one batshit crazy witch with a heart of gold and a hair-trigger temper, happened to be hanging out with some of her friends in one of the many backwater dive bars near Buttface or Asshat or *Whateversville*, West Virginia where Harmony now lives in the house she inherited from Auntie Dot.

Yes, it's true, Dot is one of the 'living impaired.' (Her definition, not mine.) She does, however, not subscribe to the old adage of resting in peace. She is the Ghostess with the mostest, still raising hell and wreaking havoc whenever she can.

Moving on, back in the day, she overheard Nate the Bastard telling his merry band of dipshits about his crazy plan to populate the earth with his spawn. (Sure, the term is offensive but most of his offspring turned out to be, well... umm...let's just say, not quite right.) After running home and telling Harmony's mom, Mary, who was pregnant with my awesome half-sister at the time, the two of them came up with the plan to banish dear old dad to CopacaNetherworld. (That's the deep dark hole stuck between Purgatory and the Pits of Hell where Witches and Wizards who messed up in epic and truly horrible ways while alive get to live out their afterlives. Think 1960's Vegas, complete with the Rat Pack, scantily clad cigarette girls, and mobsters, where the same day repeats itself over and over, you can never get drunk no matter how many Gin and Tonics you drink, and the food tastes like actual shit on an actual shingle. Colorful, but still Hell no matter how you slice it.)

Giving credit where credit is due, I have to say Dot and Mary had some real *chutzpah*. Nate the Bastard was strong, hopped up on Hades' Hellfire and stronger than three oxen and a Sumo wrestler. What they did is freaking amazing, to say the very least.

They were ready and waiting. Nate walked in the front door, the ladies cut off his head, threw a major-kick-him-in-the-ass-make-him-see-stars whammy on his skanky hide and Bob's your uncle – they were rid of the asshole. (I've never really understood that saying, but Bertie, a friend of mine from some little village in England, always says it and it seemed to fit this situation so, I gave it a try.) My sperm donor was magically thrown into the biggest club in Purgatory making the world safe from his lying, impregnating ass for what they presumed would be forever.

Of course, his assholishness didn't stop there. Unbeknownst to the ladies, during the years after he'd made his pact with Hades and before he met my mom, Nate the Bastard had been shoving a nasty little spell of his own making into every grimoire he could find. The hex or curse, whichever you prefer, was to talk Harmony into releasing him from Witchy Purgatory.

Talk about hedging your bets. The bastard really tried to think of everything. Why is it that truly awful people always come up with the most foolproof plans? Yeah, I have no clue either. Something to think about though, later, after my tale maybe.

For now, back to your regularly scheduled story...

Thanks for sticking with me. I know that explanation was long, but it was necessary, and you're about to see why. Remember back up there before I got off track on Nate the Bastard when I said it wasn't Daisy's fault that she was so tired all the time? Well, now I can tell you, and you will understand, that her mom, Cassandra, is none other than a goddess. She's the one humans call the Sandman. (I know. I was shocked too.)

But, if you think about it, she's got the best cover ever. Everyone thinks she's a tiny, little, gnome-like dude who puts people to sleep and gives them peacefully sweet dreams. When in all actuality, she could be a supermodel. (Really, the woman is gor-ge-ous. The only fault I can find is that she was conned by Nate just like all the others. Then again, he was a silver-tongued demon – *literally*.)

Now, you see why I can't get mad at Daisy for always being tired. Her internal clock doesn't kick into overdrive until about nine p.m. Good thing Rosie and I don't need a lot of sleep, because when Daisy is awake, she is A-WAKE.

"Are you listening to me, Faith?" Rosie demanded. "Or have you gone off to La-La-Land again."

"I'm listening." (I wasn't and she knew it.) "Just thinking about how to drum up some business."

As if on cue, the door behind me swung open and in pranced Portia. Her bubblegum pink tutu flounced to and fro while her flashing, bedazzled, magenta, talon-like nails made my head spin. (At that point, I was really considering an office dress code.) Sticking out her hand and dangling a piece of paper just shy of the end of my nose, the Pink Pearlescent Fairy huffed, "Henrietta says her chicken coop was vandalized and three of her best egg-layers were hen-napped. She's freakin' out and wants you to come right away."

Closing my eyes and counting to three, I prayed that it was all a bad dream, that when I reopened my lids the day would've reset. I would get a redo. Imagine that. Yeah, well, imagine no more, that crap didn't happen.

Snatching the message from my snippy secretary's fingers, I slapped on a sickeningly sweet, all be it fake, smile and smirked, "Thanks so much, Portia."

Before I could read the message, the phone was ringing once again. Fortunately, the Pink Pain-in-my-butt answered the damn thing on the second ring. Unfortunately, she screeched, "It's Henrietta again, and she's so pissed she's literally clucking between every word"

With a truly exasperated breath, I let my head fall forward as my shoulders followed suit by slumping in what I could only assume was a most unflattering way and sighed, "Just what this day needed, a six-foot-three Cajun Chicken Shifter whose about to sprout feathers and peck the ground."

Grabbing my purse and throwing back my shoulders, I added, "Come on, girls. Time to get to work."

Check Out the WHOLE STORY at JuliaMillsAuthor.com

WANNA SEE HOW THE SOUTHERN FRIED SASS LADIES CAME TO BE?

Check Out HARMONY: A 'Not-Quite' Haunted Love Story!

"Woot-woo, baby got back."

"Shut up, Ernesto. I'm not in the mood," I growled, stepping over twenty-pounds of neurotic, long-haired, Persian feline while yelling at a seventy-five-year-old toucan who was obsessed with my butt.

"Do you have to clean yourself in the middle of the hall, Wendy?" I growled. "I'm trying to get ready for a client, not to mention that your hairballs are getting' outta hand. I just cleaned one out of my favorite black Doc Martins. Can't you just throw up in the toilet like a civilized cat?"

"Yes and no," the one-eyed cat who was having her third, or maybe it was fourth, mid-life crisis of the morning, wailed. "To answer your questions in order. This spot has the best aura to reduce the stress in my chi and secondly, I refuse to put my face *anywhere near* where your butt has been."

"I'll reduce the stress in your chi," I grumbled under my breath. "With a swift kick to the backside and as for where my butt's been…"

"Back that ass up," Ernesto chimed in, perfectly imitating the rapper, Juvenile.

Before I could yell at the stupid parrot to shut his flappin' beak, I was summoned with, "Harmony, oh Harmony, are you up there?"

"Yes, Festus. Where else would I be?"

"In the back of my cage. Letting me slap that ass," Ernesto added, pushing me over the edge, way past my daily limit of bullshit.

Grabbing the thick metal bars of the parrot's humongous six-foot tall and eight-foot wide cage, I leaned in until the bars were pressed against my cheeks, put on my best 'shut-your-mouth-or-get-your-neck-wrung-and-get-plucked-look and snarled, "If you say *one* more word about my ass, I swear to the Goddess I'll make parrot pot pie and serve it to Wendy for dinner. Ya' get me?"

Waving his wings in the air, Ernesto, the bastard parrot, pleaded, "Please don't cook me. Pleeeeeease don't let Wendy eat me. I can't help it; your backside is just so…"

Snapping my fingers, I conjured the biggest carving knife I could imagine, jammed it through the bars with the point just millimeters from his eye and threatened, "Shut. Your. Beak."

Jumping to the highest perch in his cage, the foul-mouthed fowl curled into a ball, covered his head with his wings and turned his back to me. Clanking the blade of my knife against the thick, metal bars of his cage, I added, "And stay that way. I need this client. It's been ages since I've banished, summoned or bespelled anything more than a broom and dustpan. Doesn't anybody in Asscrack have ghosts but me?"

The sound of donkey hooves on my freshly polished wooden stairs caught my attention a split-second before Festus called out, "Harmony, darling, we are all out of tofu, and the alfalfa sprouts are all brown and slimy.

Letting the knife I was thinking about plunging into my own ear fade into the magical ether from where it came, I slowly turned towards the mule. With clenched fists and all the control left in my five-foot-five, curvy body, I ground out, "How would you like me to get to the store, Festus? Huh?" I threw my arms open wide. "Would you like me to fly? Get out my broom and zoom through the air?"

I took a threatening step forward, unable to control my mouth now that the floodgates were open and jabbed the index finger of my right hand towards the donkey while growling through gritted teeth, "I guess I could take my van. You know the one. It's bright pink, has a blue and white dragon painted on the side and the license plate reads, 'PNK LDY'."

Stopping three feet in front of Festus, I crossed my arms over my chest, tapped my chin with the tip of the finger I'd just been pointing at him and feigned contemplation before snarling, "But I can't, can I?"

Once again, my arms flew out to the side as I screamed like a loon. "Because you had a 'date' with Vanessa and while you were passed out on the lawn after she blew your mind with her nookie skills, she and her pony pals stole my beautiful Pink Lady and took off for parts unknown."

"Now, darling," the voice of my Aunt Dot whistled through the hall a few seconds before her image appeared, hovering overhead, luckily for her just out of my reach. "You know that wasn't Festus' fault. Vanessa was and is his first love. How was he to know she was going to boink him silly and commit grand theft auto?"

"How was he to know?!" I yelled, spinning towards my aunt but stopping short to glare at the other ghost in the room, Sampson, Sam to most, who had just opened his mouth, "Do *not* say a word. I need no help from you, Buster," I scarily warned, before continuing to turn around.

Looking back to my not-so dearly-departed aunt, I continued, "How the hell was Festus not to know, Dot?! Better yet, why in all that is unholy was he doing the horizontal donkey hokey-pokey in my van?" I blocked the illicit images threatening to run through my mind with a violent shake of my head and gulped a deep breath in an attempt to lower my temperature, my blood pressure, and the big fiery-red ball of angry magic floating to the side of my head.

Letting out the breath I was holding, I tersely advised, "All of you need to go away, hide, get out of my sight until after Mr. and Mrs. Andrews have come and gone. They're coming for a consultation for the removal of spirits from their home and I really want to get back to work." I slowly looked every single being in my house in the eyes, before slowly (Think talking to a group of preschoolers who just had a bag of sweet tarts and a gallon of red Kool-Aid.) explaining, "And if they see *you* lot, I can't begin to fathom the rumors that will be flying around Asscrack. Imagine this as the lead story on the evening news, Psychotic Witch, Kills Three Crazy Animals and Two Ghosts, film at eleven."

"Dear, I hate to point out..."

Ignoring my aunt's retort and powering on, "Not to mention, you two," I pointed at said auntie and her partner in crime, Sam. "Are bad for business. How can I convince people I'm good at exorcising spirits with you two floating around like it's Casper's Day Camp?"

"But Harmony, you know you have to *want* to banish a ghost to be able to banish a ghost." Dot's shoulder-length, gray, corkscrew curls bounced up and down as she tilted her head to the side and shrugged. Holding out her arms, beckoning me in for a hug while I stood my ground, absolutely refusing to fall for her lovey-dovey BS, I listened as she added, "And somewhere in that big, wonderful heart of yours, you know you don't want to be rid of either one of us."

Rolling my eyes and heading towards my room, I grumbled over my shoulder, "Oh, trust me. I want you gone. I just haven't found a spell strong enough, but when I do..."

Not willing to finish my declaration and have both Sam and Aunt Dot moping around, I slammed the heavy, oak door of my bedroom to escape the madness and stalked to the closet. Grabbing my favorite orange T-shirt adorned with a sequined witch's hat atop a cute little jack-o-lantern, black jeans and black, denim jacket off their hangers, I went about getting ready for my appointment while trying to block out the fiasco from a few minutes ago. It wasn't that I didn't love the mixed-up, bat-shit crazy, dysfunctional band of misfits that I called family, I really did, but enough is enough.

I had almost gotten my blood pressure back to normal and the pounding in my head to a dull roar when the scent of Raleigh Light 100's and Chantilly perfume wafted through the room. Yippee, Aunt Dot was making another uninvited appearance.

Stepping into the bathroom, ignoring the hovering image of my favorite relative, I brushed my long, brown, wavy locks and put it up in my trademark ponytails with the new orange and black hair ties I'd ordered from Amazon. Taking off my glasses and laying them on the counter, I slapped some powder over the multitude of freckles that dotted my peaches and cream complexion and leaned in close to the mirror make sure it was even.

"I need to do something to brighten up these dark eyes," I mumbled to myself, getting the mascara out of the drawer and brushing it on my long, dark lashes. "And just a little bit of blush, too, I think," I added, still effectively ignoring my aunt while also making myself feel better. (And that's how you multi-task, girls.)

Looking at myself in the mirror, happy with the way my outfit hid the curves I didn't like and accentuated the ones I did, I put on a thin layer of my favorite burnt honey lip gloss, slid my glasses back on and headed out of the room. Thankfully, all the patients of Harmony's Hospital for the Harried had taken my earlier hint (Read that as command.) and were either hiding under the furniture or completely gone from sight.

Hopping down the steps, my mood magically lightened the closer I got to my office. Opening the French doors, the long plates of glass etched with a dragon flying across a full moon, the scent of sage, cedar, sweetgrass and lavender beckoned me in. Not only was my space sacred and cleansed, but it was welcoming and inviting. Continuing to take deep inhales and long slow exhales, I made my way to the circular, mirrored-topped granite table, taking a seat in my favorite high back chair, and sinking my pleasantly-rounded behind into the fluffy, red velvet cushion.

Closing my eyes, I sat silently, feeling the beautiful, white magic of my ancestors filling my spirit. Pink bubbles and purples stars burst to life behind my eyelids as all the stress of dealing with my 'family' faded away. Relaxed and ready for my appointment, not even the scent of cigarette smoke and old witch perfume dampened my spirits as the doorbell outside the separate entrance to my business chimed the melody of 'That Old Black Magic'.

Opening the painted red wooden door, I smiled at the nervous couple on my doorstep who stood arm-in-arm, holding one another up, and beamed, "Welcome." Taking a step back, I swept my hand to the side and added, "Come on in. There's freshly brewed tea on the table and some home-made pumpkin cookies."

Following the couple, as they *ever so slowly* made their way to the table in the middle of what used to be Auntie Dot's massive and severely underused library, I had to hold back a chuckle while they looked around every corner and under damn near every piece of furniture before taking a seat. Pouring their tea, I chattered away, trying to make them more comfortable and failing miserably, before giving up on easing their tensions, sitting down and straight-forwardly asking, "So, tell me about the last time you tried to have the spirits in your house removed."

The skin under Mr. Andrew's combover immediately turned a brilliant shade of red at the precise moment that all the color drained from his wife's face. Watching carefully as they looked at one another then at their hands then at me, I smiled as sweetly as possible and added, "I know there are a lot of charlatans out there, so please don't be embarrassed. I just asked so that I can gauge how much you truly know about the spirit world."

"Harmony, something's not right," Auntie Dot's voice floated through my mind.

"Get outta here. You're gonna scare away the paying customers."

"Harmony Jane, you listen to me." Using her magic, my dear old auntie whopped me on the back of the head while commanding, *"Open your eyes, girl. Look at what's right in front of you."*

"Aunt Dot, get the..."

The rest of my snappy comeback was stolen from my lips as Mr. and Mrs. Andrews' bodies melted away like the wax on a burning candle only to immediately be replaced by two cackling, squealing, poltergeists dressed like Al Capone and arguing like teenage girls. "Where did the dame go? We gots to bump her off before Johnny Law finds out about the boss' stash of hooch," the tall, thin guy with a long nose and sunken eyes demanded.

"I dunno," the short, round man with bulging eyes and a dark wool flat cap shrugged. "But I ain't goin' to the big house for Mikey's mistake. Ain't no skirt worth all that."

Stunned speechless, I watched as they walked around my office talking like it was any normal day, picking up even the smallest crystals on the shelves looking for the woman who 'ratted' them out to the police. Finally snapping out of my trance while shutting out Auntie Dot's recriminating taunts of, *"I told you so. You just never listen to me,"* I tapped the mirror that served as a tabletop and watched as the refreshments popped out of existence.

Pink bubbles and purple sparks surrounded by bright yellow smoke floated over my head as thick white clouds swirled in the depths of the looking glass that dated back to the Salem Witch trials, or what my ancestors like to call our Coming Out Party. Clapping my hands, I winked at the awestruck ghosts who in that very moment realized they weren't alone as I teased, "Whatcha boys doin' here?"

Stepping towards me like I figured they would, (Did I mention they were both a couple pumpkins shy of a patch?) the phantoms asked in unison, "Are you the broad? The one what's ratted out the boss?"

"No, boys. I'm not the *broad*." I grinned, wrinkled my nose, and added a wink for good measure as I got to my feet. "I'm the witch what's throwing your asses back where you came from." Raising my hands, I chanted, "It's off to the Twenties you go. Out of my house and out of my sight. Into the mirror and back across time, have a good flight and get outta here."

My magical pink bubbles burst like firecrackers on the Fourth of July while purple stars cascaded from the ceiling resembling a sparkling waterfall as the two gangsters were sucked into the looking glass, spinning and whirling round and round before disappearing like suds down a drain. A loud pop shook the windows in their frames and threw me back into my seat as rainbow glitter floated to the ground while my ears rang like church bells on Easter Sunday.

No sooner had my hearing cleared than the bell on the front door chimed 'Ding Dong the Witch is Dead' (Yes. I have two doorbells. This place is huge, and I thought it was cool. Sue me.) and Aunt Dot announced, "It's your friend Lola, and she's got Zelda with her." Her face instantly appeared before me as I walked towards the foyer. Sticking out her tongue and blowing me a raspberry, she taunted, "Hope Zelda doesn't report you to the Baba Yaga or better yet sentence you herself for cruelty to your ancestors, namely me." She harrumphed. "You won't last a minute in the magical pokey."

Snapping my fingers and smiling as Auntie Dot was whisked into the basement, locked inside the brass urn I'd bespelled to hold her - well, at least for a little while - I opened the door and smiled, "You two sure have some shit timing. Come on in. Join the party. You're never gonna believe what just happened to me."

Check Out the WHOLE STORY at JuliaMillsAuthor.com

READ ALL OF THE SOUTHER FRIED SASS STORIES!

Welcome to Hairy Wart!
Home of the SOUTHERN FRIED SASS DETECTIVE
AGENCY and the DRAGONETTES.
Those bite-size Dragons are proof that it's not the size of the
scales but the SASS in the Flames that makes the
Guardsma...*ahem*, I mean **GUARDSWOMAN!**

Check Out the WHOLE SERIES at JuliaMillsAuthor.com

Later Gator
Lazy Daisy
Nosey Rosie
Jamie's Got A Wand
and...
COMING SOON
Kerri, Kerri Quite Contrary!

"Dammit, Grace, pick up the phone," she growled through gritted teeth at the third voicemail she'd had to listen to in the last five minutes.

"Everything okay, Kyndel?' Barney, the *nice* guy in her office, asked.

"Yeah, everything's fine. Just trying to find Grace."

"Oh! Anything I can help with?"

Kyndel thought about telling him her troubles, but Barney had been spending an excessive amount of time in her office lately. At first, she'd thought he was just being nice, but then he joined her hiking group, and just yesterday he showed up with her favorite no whip, nonfat, iced white chocolate mocha from the *frou-frou* coffee shop on the corner. It had been then Kyndel realized she was Barney's newest crush. It had been a long time between boyfriends and Barney was nice, but...um...*no*. As flattered as she was, there was no way she had an office romance.

'Don't shit where you eat' was one of the pieces of sage advice Granny had given her just after graduation. Not that it ever truly made sense to Kyndel, but she got the gist of it... keep your personal life *out* of the office.

She saw the puppy dog look on Barney's face and hated to crush his spirit, but Kyndel decided a brisk walk home would be better than leading the poor fellow on, in *any* way.

"No but thank you so much." Then, to make sure he got the hint and skedaddled, she added, "Have a nice a weekend," before turning her chair and dialing Grace's office for the third time.

Voicemail *again*. Time to pack up and get the heck outta dodge before someone found something else for her to do. Bag on shoulder, scowl on face, and more than a little disgusted, Kyndel headed out of the office.

*Never loan Grace the car... Never loan Grace the car...*was the mantra playing on a loop in Kyndel's mind. She was madder than a wet hen and getting hotter by the minute. It was *no fun* to walk home after ten hours of work. *No fun* to be abandoned and forgotten by the best friend she'd loaned her car to. *No fun* to make the five-block journey past the park...in the dark.

At twenty-six, she rarely admitted her fear of the dark and held her aunts responsible for the phobia. Had they not made her watch 'The Brain Eaters' when she was only six years old, Kyndel was positive everything would've been just fine. It wasn't that she believed aliens would set loose a horde of parasites to eat every human brain on the planet; she had a *little* more sense than that. It was the feeling of being watched...like someone was hiding in the shadows, just waiting for an opportunity to scare the living daylights out of her. At the mere thought of her' phantom stalker', the hair stood up at the nape of her neck, and she walked a bit faster.

A sudden *thud,* and what sounded like footsteps pounding on the hard ground, had her stopping in her tracks. "What the...?" She gasped, opening her eyes wide, hoping it would help her see through the shadows.

Several tense seconds later—that felt like damn near forever—and Kyndel moved again. This time, her eyes slid side-to-side like the stupid black and white cat clock her granny used to have in the kitchen.

The farther she got from where she'd heard the 'thump,' the easier it was to convince herself it had just been kids sneaking into the park after hours. Manlove Park was a popular make-out spot for teenagers. There might've even been a time after moving to the city when Kyndel herself had been convinced to take a walk on the wild side, but that was a story for another day.

Shoot, now I wouldn't know the wild side if I tripped and fell in it.

It had been almost a year since she'd dated the muscle-headed jock from the gym. Three long, tortuous dates and all because he had an incredible body. Of course, dating the douche bag had come at a price. She'd spent the entire time listening to him drone on about his body parts...*and not the good ones*...and *only* when he wasn't checking out every other woman in the joint.

It wasn't that he'd hurt her feelings. Kyndel knew who she was and had never been under the misconception she would be Miss America. She had a few extra pounds, and her curves had curves, but she was cute and had a brain, something not everyone could claim. What had pissed her off the most about dating Vinnie was, she'd wasted three whole evenings of her life that she could never get back. The one compliment the jerk had given her had been about her skin; he thought it was beautiful. Her granny always called her complexion peaches and cream and said her freckles added character.

Yeah, cause I need more of that.

She sighed as she thought about how much of her youth she'd wasted hating those tiny brown spots, until the day she realized they weren't going anywhere. It was time to buck up and learn to love them or stop looking in the mirror. From that day forward, she stopped using makeup to cover them and embraced her 'freckled-self.' She also learned to accept her curves. *If ya don't like 'em, don't look at 'em* was her motto. For the most part, she ate right and worked out at least three times a week. But dammit if she didn't love her Ben and Jerry's Cherry Garcia and someone would lose a hand if they tried to take it from her.

A loud *'thud'* echoed between the buildings. Kyndel stumbled to a stop. She looked and listened. The longer she thought about what she'd heard, the easier it was for her to convince herself someone had yelled for help. So, for the second time in about as many minutes, she searched the inky shadows for signs of life. Her anxiety level quadrupled the longer she stood still. She wanted to scream when only the sound of leaves rustling across the sidewalk and the occasional car passing by reached her ears.

Disgusted, she grumbled aloud, "You've gone bonkers, Kyn." The sound of her own voice somehow calmed her rankled nerves, and she added, "Get to stepping, girlie."

The clicking of her heels bounced off the brick wall of the library as she hurried past. Resuming her original mantra, she added *Must kill Grace* at the end for good measure.

"I swear when I get my hands on..."

Her words were cut short as the unmistakable sound of a man groaning came from the shadows.

A chill skittered down her spine.

Goosebumps covered her arms.

She counted to three, unable to move...simply listening...praying it was only her imagination. One deep breath later, she slid her right foot forward, prepared to make a beeline for home at a high rate of speed.

The groan came again. Closer than before. More desperate...almost pleading.

The need to help the injured grew within her. Turning towards the darkness, Kyndel searched for the source of the noise.

Shaking so much her teeth chattered, she looked for any sign of the man she *knew* needed her help.

"It's time to make a decision, Kyndel. Fight or flight. What's it gonna be? God knows, standing like a bump on a log isn't solving a *damn* thing."

Flight won. She turned, almost running, her satchel clutched tightly to her side like a lifeline.

"Keep your head up and eyes front. Home's only a few blocks away," she reassured herself, with the promise of snatching her best friend bald for the stupid mess she was in.

Feeling guilty and worried for Grace, her heart at war with her brain, Kyndel thought aloud, "Hope everything's okay..."

Grace had always been a little scatter-brained, but she'd never just *forgotten* Kyndel before. It bothered her that there'd been no answer at Grace's office or on her cellphone when Kyndel had tried to track her down before leaving the office. She'd even taken a chance and tried her own home because Grace had a key, but only got voicemail there, too. It was a war between anger and worry that accompanied most of her thoughts about her friend lately.

The running joke was that Grace spent most of her time hooking up with eligible bachelors she met at work. The good Lord *knew* her bestie was gorgeous; five foot nine, long raven hair, blue eyes, and a curvy body without an extra ounce of fat. To top it off, she was a first-year lawyer, with a promising career. Grace had it all...brains and beauty, the total package.

Giggling nervously, she gave herself a mental swat to the back of the head. She didn't want anything bad to happen to Grace, just a bump or bruise, even a hangnail would explain being left. If she really had just forgotten, Kyndel was going to be *pissed* and more than a little hurt.

The shadows seemed to be closing in. Fear pushed Kyndel until she was almost jogging in her sensible work heels. Looking over her shoulder, the toe of her shoe caught an uneven piece of concrete, and from one heartbeat to the next, she was falling forward. Arms flailing, mouth stretched wide in a wordless scream, the sidewalk racing toward her face, everything around her seemed to happen in slow motion. All she could think was *that's gonna leave a mark.*

Bracing for impact, she squeezed her eyes tight and prayed...then nothing happened. Opening one eye, then the other, Kyndel found herself hanging above the sidewalk, looking at a pair of the biggest feet she had ever seen—and they were sexy.

Sexy feet? I really am losing it. Wait! Why the hell am I above the concrete?

Warmth radiated from the perfectly muscled arm

wrapped around her midsection. Goosebumps emanated from the extra-large hand holding firmly to her blouse, just a little too close to her breast.

She wiggled to change position, the cushion of her well-rounded ass finding the ridges of an incredibly hard set of abs. She trembled. Her heart raced. Just the thought of the man that could hold her upright made up for all her previous mishaps.

Within just a few seconds, Kyndel's world turned on its axis. The scenery blurred as she was effortlessly spun around and immediately found herself sitting atop the body of her rescuer, looking at faded denim covering extremely muscular thighs. Laughing aloud, she asked herself, *wonder what part I'll see next?*

The same muscled arm that had saved her face from inevitable demise now kept her upright. She did a one-eighty, draped her legs over his thighs, with her knees barely touching the sidewalk, and got her first look at the top half of her rescuer. All she could do was gape. He was absolutely the most handsome man she'd ever seen, with features that looked like they'd been carved by expert hands.

Even with his eyes closed, he gave off the distinctive air of authority. The dim light highlighted his high cheekbones and aristocratic nose, adding to the power she felt radiating from his every pore. His perfectly formed lips made visions of passionate kisses and hot, sweaty nights dance through her brain. It didn't help that all he had on was a pair of well-worn blue jeans.

She imagined that denim riding low on his tapered hips when he stood, highlighting the incredibly sexy dimples that sat on the front of his hips. She absolutely knew without looking they were there, and that simple bit of knowledge made her temperature rise another degree, despite the cool breeze.

At the touch of her fingertips against the cool skin of his neck, an electric current arced between them. Flashes of light burst before her eyes. She blinked to clear her vision, then felt for his pulse, strong and steady against her digit. Heat rose from his skin, making her worry he might have a fever. Her eyes wandered down his well-toned body. She scoffed, unsuccessfully trying to convince herself she was only checking for further injury.

Who the hell do you think you're fooling?

She continued her perusal, taking note of his massive shoulders and a chest that could've been sculpted from granite. The light smattering of hair that glistened in the shards of light from the streetlamps emphasized his nipples, which were pebbled from the cool breeze. Her mouth watered, and her pulse raced.

What the hell is it about this guy? Is he doused in pheromones? Or am I in heat?

Her eyes landed on the best set of abs she'd ever seen. Unable, or maybe it was unwilling, to stop her hand, she traced the defined lines of his eight-pack, mesmerized by the feel of his skin beneath her fingers. The electricity continued to flow between them. The sound of a horn in the distance pulled her from her musing and brought her current situation into the glaring light of reality. The sexy man that had kept her from breaking her face on the concrete was out cold, and she was paying him back by sitting on his lap and copping a feel.

She scrambled to her feet, surprised her rescuer hadn't moved an inch during her less than graceful attempt to remove her butt from his lap. But there he lay, unmoving, except for the rise and fall of his chest. The longer he remained unconscious, the more panicked she became.

Looking up and down the street and cursing Grace for the hundredth time, Kyndel wished for her car. First Aid class had taught her *never* to move an injured person unless you knew what was wrong. Not that she could pick him up and carry him, anyway. The dude was *HUGE*. At least six-foot-three or four, and his muscles had muscles. She prayed he hadn't hit his head on the sidewalk. A concussion could be really bad if not treated.

"You're worried about a concussion now?" She scolded herself. "You've been drooling over the guy while his head is lying on the cold, hard sidewalk. Brilliant, Kyn, just brilliant." Reaching for her satchel, she grabbed her old sorority sweatshirt from inside, wadded it up, and knelt forward to lift his head.

Her fingers tangled in his soft, brown hair. The scattered shards of light made it look like melted chocolate flowing over her skin.

Would it shine in the sun or maybe have highlights? Some lighter brown mixed with red, even a few blond streaks woven throughout?

The silky softness of his tresses turned to something wet and sticky.

Blood!

Kyndel gulped. Panic seized the breath in her lungs as the true severity of the situation smacked her in the face. She fought to keep her calm. Now, there was absolutely no denying he needed medical attention. Reaching into her bag and cursing herself for not thinking of it sooner, she dug around for her cellphone.

Coming up empty-handed, she instantly remembered plugging it into her car charger the night before, not giving it the slightest thought until that moment. Cursing and threatening death to anyone in the immediate vicinity, she sat back on her heels and thought.

All I know to do is run down the street for help.

Looking at the fallen man, then in the direction of the Mini Mart, she reasoned he'd probably be okay. She'd be gone five minutes...*tops*. Run in, use the phone, run back. It all seemed very logical, but fear something would happen to him in her absence kept her in place.

This guy was important to her. That alone had all her red flags flying and bells and whistles screaming in her brain. She tried to push her feelings aside and look at the situation with logic, but that was like holding back a freight train with her pinky finger...*not gonna happen*. Besides, her granny would most definitely haunt her and probably kick her butt if she turned her back on someone who needed help.

"No one's gonna mess with this behemoth, even if he *is* unconscious," she reassured herself. "He probably doesn't have a wallet to steal anyway."

Should she dig in his pockets to try to find one? Some kind of ID?

Nah.

She wasn't keen on trying to explain her hand in his pants if he woke up. Her cheeks warmed at the thought of touching him again.

"What are you doing out at night in just a pair of jeans and bare feet, anyway?" she asked the unconscious man. "Guess it doesn't matter. You need help, whether you're dressed properly or not."

Hooking her satchel over her shoulder, Kyndel stood and took one last look at her 'patient.' Before she had barely moved an inch, a large, warm hand latched onto her bare ankle.

"What the hell?" she screamed, trying to pull her leg free while looking down to see what new fresh hell had befallen her.

ABOUT JULIA

Find all my stories at JuliaMillsAuthor.com!
Hey Y'all! I'm Julia Mills, the New York Times and USA Today Bestselling Author of the Dragon Guard Series. I, without a doubt, admit to being a sarcastic, southern woman who would rather spend all day laughing than a minute crying. Living with my two most amazing daughters and a menagerie of animals keeps me busy, but I love telling a good story. Now that I've decided to write the stories running through my brain, life is just a blast!

My beliefs are simple. A good book, along with shoes, makeup, and purses, will never let a girl down, and no hero ever written will compare to my real-life hero, my dad! I'm a sucker for a happy ending, and alpha men make me swoon. I'm still working on my story, but I promise it will contain as much love and laughter as I can pack into it!

Now, go out there and create your own story! Dare to Dream! Have the Strength to Try EVERYTHING! Never Look Back!

I ABSOLUTELY adore stalkers, so look me up on Facebook,

sign up for my newsletter at JuliaMillsAuthor.com, and
follow me on BookBub.
Send me a message!
XOXO Julia

ALSO BY JULIA MILLS

Find Them All at JuliaMillsAuthor.com!

Although this epic journey travels through many Clans, many lands, and many couples, one thing remains constant :

Fate Will Not Be Denied!

Each book is written as a standalone story, but just like M&M's, Lay's Potato Chips, and my momma's queso, they're better when binged.

Dragon Guard Order

1.Her Dragon to Slay

2.Her Dragon's Fire

3.Haunted by Her Dragon

4.For the Love of Her Dragon

5.Saved by Her Dragon

Her Love, Her Dragon, A Dragon Guard Prequel

6.Only for Her Dragon

7.Fighting for Her Dragon

8.Her Dragon's Heart

9.Her Dragon's Soul

10.The Fate of Her Dragon

11.Her Dragon's No Angel

Dragon Guard Collections

Dragon Intelligence Agency

Dragon Guard Berserkers

Banning

Asher

Raynor

Dragon Guard Berserkers, Volume 1

Ladies of the Sky

Sadie's Shadow

Kings of the Blood

Viktor

Roman

Achilles

Kings of the Blood, Books 1 - 3

Dragons of Fate

Chestnuts Roasting Over Dragon Fire

Unwrapping Her Dragon

She Needs A Little Dragon

Falling Off Her Dragon

The Dragon of Valentine's Past

Dragons of Fate Collection, Books 1 - 4

Dragon of Destiny

Dragon Him Out To Sea

Dragon Guard Holiday Love Stories

It's The Great Dragon, Molly Brown

A Little Elfin' Around

Heart On For Dragon

Dragons Fall Hard

Dragon Guard Holiday Love Stories, Books 1 -3

Not Quite Holiday Love Stories

Kissing Cupid

Kissing Claws

Maidens of Mayhem

That Hound Don't Hunt

That Pig Gonna Fly

That Mule's Got A Kick

That Rex Gotta Roar

That Shark is Red Hot

That Dino's Hanging Ten

That Dragon Gonna Blow

Not Quite Love Stories

Vidalia

Phoebe

Zoey

Jax

Heidi

Lola

Sammie Jo

Harmony

Daphne

Magic & Mayhem Collections

The Not Quite Collection Volume 1

The Not Quite Collection Volume 2

Maidens of Mayhem Collection Volume 3

Maidens of Mayhem Collection Volume 4

Southern Fried Sass

Later Gator

Nosey Rosie

Lazy Daisy

Jamie's Got A Wand

Southern Fried Sass: Volume 1

Coloring Books

Bitch Please! I Color Dragons

Witch Please! I Color Dragons

Dragons of Legend Coloring Book

Planners

The Dragon Never Sleeps

No Rest for The Dragon

Reading Journals

On the Wings of Words

JOIN THE CLAN!

Wanna keep up with all my crazy? Have fun? Win some cool
prizes? Get exclusive excerpts of upcoming books?
Sign up for my newsletter at JuliaMillsAuthor.com.
Be the FIRST to see new covers, sneak peeks, and, best of
all, ADVANCED COPIES OF ALL MY BOOKS and
REVIEW COPIES OF ALL MY AUDIOBOOKS!!!
Join the group! Julia's Mills' Fan Club on Facebook!
I absolutely LOVE stalkers! Follow me everywhere!
Website
Facebook
Instagram
TikTok
Pinterest
BookBub
Goodreads

SOUTHERN FRIED SASS

Julia Mills
.SASSY.
10 Years & Still Flying High
WWW.JULIAMILLSAUTHOR.COM